HER COWBOY BILLIONAIRE BOSS

A WHITTAKER BROTHERS NOVEL, CHRISTMAS IN CORAL CANYON BOOK 2

LIZ ISAACSON

AEJ
CREATIVE WORKS

ONE

ELI WHITTAKER STOOD at the window, watching the snow drift down. While this was a pretty fancy lodge, with all the best materials, he could still hear the excited squeals of his son, Stockton.

Moving to Wyoming was definitely the right thing to do, and Eli was glad he'd done it. Relieved to be closer to family, who could help him with his son, though he had Meg for that.

Meg Palmer, the best nanny in the world—at least according to his six-year-old.

Eli sighed and turned away from the glass as it fogged from his breath.

Meg. What was he going to do about Meg?

"Don't need to do anything," he muttered to himself as he moved through the large master suite and out the door.

He walked a few steps down the hall and into the office he shared with his brother.

Graham had not arrived yet, something that meant he was eternally happy with his wife, step-daughter, and the new baby that would be here by summer.

Eli exhaled again as he sat at his desk, in no mood to try to get more people up to the lodge for snowshoeing and Christmas tree cutting. He'd been back in Coral Canyon for eleven months now, and he hadn't had a problem getting tourists and locals alike up to the lodge in the spring, summer, and fall.

But winter was another beast altogether, and Eli wondered if he ought to just take the season off. But as it happened to last for months on end, he honestly wouldn't know what to do with himself.

His thoughts wandered as they were wont to do when he didn't have something big to focus on. And these days, they went straight to Meg and lingered there. Ever since she'd found him late on Thanksgiving Day and told him she had real feelings for him, Eli hadn't known how to act around her.

Someone knocked on the office door, and from the light, hesitant nature of it, he felt sure it would be the woman who'd been plaguing him for months now. Yes, months. A lot longer than just the few weeks since Thanksgiving.

"Yeah, come in," he said, because ignoring problems was Eli Whittaker's specialty. Meg hadn't brought up her crush again—in fact, she'd told Eli to forget she'd said anything.

She entered the office carrying a tray with coffee and toast, a quick, nervous smile on her face. That had definitely changed—the way she seemed so anxious around him now—but Eli didn't know what to do about it.

"Celia asked me to bring you this." She took one, two, three steps, and her foot caught on the edge of the rug.

Everything happened so quickly and yet so slowly at the same time. Gravity grabbed onto Meg, a petite woman, and pulled her down fast. Panic crossed her face and her knees hit before Eli could even move a muscle.

Since she had the tray in her hands, she couldn't catch herself. Hot coffee splashed his jeans in the same moment her elbows hit the hardwood, and then her face.

Time spun forward, and Eli leapt to her aid, his skin bristling a bit at the hot liquid soaking into his pants, shoes, and the rug.

"Meg." His heart reverberated through his whole body, bouncing against the back of his throat. "Are you okay?"

What a stupid question. As she righted herself by rolling onto her backside, pain flashed in her eyes, and she cradled her face with her now-free hand. Tears appeared, and she turned those beautiful, dark eyes away from him.

"I'm fine."

She wasn't fine, and Eli put his hand on her elbow. The simple touch sent fire flowing through him, and he pulled his hand back. So he had a crush on his nanny too and had for a few months now.

But she was his *nanny*, and he wasn't going to be one of those men who fell for a woman because his kid loved her so much.

Meg tucked her dark hair behind her ear and slid away from him.

"Let me—"

"I'm fine, Eli. I'll tell Celia about your breakfast." She used his desk to support herself as she got to her feet, and she limped out of the office while Eli stared after her.

He hung his head, wishing he could go back in time and change how he'd handled things at Thanksgiving. He'd made a right mess of things between him and Meg, and he was actually quite surprised she hadn't found another job.

Celia arrived just as Eli picked up the fallen toast and coffee cup. "Are you okay, sir?"

"Don't call me sir." He told her that every day, and yet she continued to address him in such a formal manner. It felt weird coming from the woman he'd known his whole life, who used to serve him pancakes at the diner.

"You sign my checks."

"I do not. Graham does that."

Celia tilted her head and reached for the tray. She took the dishes and toast and set them on it. "I'll get Annie in here straightaway. And I'll set more toast for you."

Eli focused on the dark stain on the rug. "How's Meg?" he asked.

"She's...disappeared into her room." Celia turned back toward the doorway. "I'll check on her in a minute."

"I'll do it," Eli said.

Celia gave him a quick glance over her shoulder but said nothing other than, "Stockton's in the basement with Andrew."

"Thank you," Eli murmured, his attention already wandering down the hall and around the corner, past the master suite, to the bedroom in the corner of the lodge where Meg lived. She had two days off every week, and today was one of them. Dared he go and check on her?

"Only if you're going to say more than three words to her," he lectured himself. Their conversations, which used to be so lively and a bright spot in his day, had become stiff. And he hated that more than anything.

In this lodge, with a cook, a housekeeper, a decorator, his brother, his nanny, and his son, Eli felt utterly alone. So lonely. When Graham showed up in the office, he and Eli sometimes talked about something besides the lodge, the horses, or Springside Energy, the family company Graham ran.

Eli had always been able to count on Meg providing a few minutes of laughter, a ray of sunshine. Now, he had hardly anything to remind him what was good about the world.

Caroline.

Caroline.

Caroline.

The name haunted him as he walked slowly out of the office, down the hall, and around the corner. He couldn't believe he'd used his first wife as a shield against his own feelings for Meg.

She'd nodded and clenched her hands together when he'd said his late wife's name on Thanksgiving. "I understand," she'd said, but even Eli didn't understand so he wasn't sure how Meg could.

"Meg?" He knocked on her bedroom door. She had a suite too, though not as large as the master. "It's Eli, and I just want to make sure you're all right." He couldn't hear anything behind her door, not even a sniffle.

He tried the doorknob, and it wasn't locked, so he gently pushed open the door. "Meg, I'm coming in."

The door swung wide and he took a slow step inside, locating her in the armchair next to the bay window, facing away from him. The sniffling met his ears now, and he hesitated. "Meg?"

"I'm really fine," she said.

"You hit your face." Four words. He'd gotten up to four words. He crept closer, noting that her room was absolutely spotless. She was organized, punctual, and practically perfect in every way. It was no wonder Eli had started feeling soft things for her.

With her dark hair and dark eyes, quick smile and keen intelligence, Eli had liked Meg from the moment he'd met her. Four years ago now since he'd been looking for a nanny after the death of his wife.

Stockton had only been two years old when Caroline had died, and Eli spent a lot of time making sure the boy knew who his mother was. But she was fading inside Eli's mind too, and a pinch started in his stomach.

A pinch that would grow, expand, swell until it consumed him. He'd had so little time with her, and he'd loved her so very much.

He honestly didn't know if he could love someone else as much as he'd loved her, wasn't even sure he could love another woman. But Meg had made him start to question all of that, and Caroline had been fading faster and faster since his return to Coral Canyon.

"Can I bring you some painkillers?" Eli asked. "A cold bottle of water? Some ice?"

She kept her face turned away from him, softly crying. She pulled in a deep breath in an obvious attempt to calm down. "I'll take all of those."

With a purpose, he turned to go do as requested. But he turned back to her and rounded the armchair so he faced her. He bent down and ran his fingertips down the side of her face. "I'm so sorry, Meg. Are you sure you're okay?"

She lifted those beautiful eyes to his and said, "I think I'm just in shock, you know? I've never fallen flat on my face before." Fresh tears slithered down her cheeks, and he wiped them away on her non-injured side.

"I'll get your pills and the ice. You can come sit by me in the office." It felt so nice to talk to her like normal again.

She shook her head, agony making her face crumple. Eli wanted to take her pain and endure it for her, and he hated that he couldn't do anything. But he could. Get the pills, the water, and the ice.

"I just want to stay here," she said. "Until I feel less shaky."

"I'll be right back then." He pulled her door closed behind him though her room was about as far out of the way as a room could get. He found Celia in the kitchen with a bag of ice all ready to go.

Eli selected a bottle of water from the fridge and shook four painkillers into his palm from the bottle in the cupboard beside the fridge. "She's okay," he said. "She's going to stay in her room and rest for a while."

"Good idea." Celia flipped a page in the cookbook in front of her. Eli started to leave when she added, "And Eli, talk to her, please. She's so miserable."

Eli blinked at the older woman. "I talk to her."

"You know what I mean." She rolled her eyes and turned another page.

Eli left her in the kitchen, took the items to Meg, and retreated back to his master bedroom so he could call his mother in private.

"Mom," he said when she picked up. "I need your advice." He cleared his throat. He'd always been very close to his mother, but it had been a while since Eli had needed her quite so badly.

"Advice about what, dear? Is Stockton okay?"

Eli half laughed and half exhaled. It would be so easy to just ask something about Stockton, hang up, and go sit back at his desk.

Instead, he said, "No, it's not about Stockton. It's about a woman."

"A woman?" The curiosity in her voice filled the whole room.

Eli sat down on the bed heavily, his heart feeling as though someone had filled it with cement. "I feel like I'm being disloyal to Caroline, but I like this other woman, and I don't know what to do about any of it."

TWO

MEG'S FACE HURT. She finally got herself to stop hiccupping, the tears dry and cracked on her cheeks now. She was exceedingly glad she didn't have Stockton today, because she didn't like showing the boy anything but fun and games and joy.

The hint of Eli's cologne still hung in the air—or maybe Meg just had the scent memorized and enjoyed it so much she could always smell it.

No matter what, her crush on him had roared back to full force when they'd come to Wyoming. She'd always had a soft spot for men in cowboy hats, wearing cowboy boots, and those jeans....

He worked with horses now, too, which was totally unfair. He had so many skills, and she had absolutely no defense against his charm, his good looks, and now his cowboy hat and easy way with animals.

She'd thought she could be honest with him, that some of the moments they'd shared in the eleven months they'd been in Wyoming couldn't have just been one-sided. She couldn't have been the only one feeling sparks, butterflies, heat.

Could she?

So she'd spoken up, and wow, that had gone badly.

She turned away from the window, wishing she could turn away from her thoughts as easily. "Should've known you couldn't compete with his dead wife." Meg tucked her hair behind her ears, accidentally touching her cheekbone. A sharp pain swept down her jaw, causing tears to prick her eyes again.

She pushed those away too and pulled her comforter down. It was torture sleeping on this side of the wall when she knew Eli was just on the other side. Well, his master closet was, with the huge master bath. And then his bedroom. But he was right there, selecting the perfect pair of jeans and the pink, yellow, and blue checkered shirt that made her throat dry and her pulse pound.

She lay down and pulled the blanket to her chin. The painkillers he'd brought her a half an hour ago were starting to kick in, and Meg felt certain as soon as she woke up from her nap, everything in the world would be fixed.

Another fantasy, but Meg entertained it anyway. After all, she didn't have much else to sustain her, and she often lived inside games of pretend when dealing with children.

She woke, instinctively aware that someone had

entered her room. A quick breath in, and Meg groaned and moved. Her teeth ached, and she had no idea why.

"Meggy?"

"Stockton?" She opened her eyes and tried to sit up, but her legs were too tangled in the blankets.

"Stockton." Eli appeared in the doorway, his voice firm. "I said she was resting."

"I just wanted to see." The little boy climbed right into bed with Meg and peered into her face, his eyes so much like his father's it made Meg's chest pinch. That deep hazel that could never be replicated with crayons, with such bright flecks of green.

"Daddy said you fell."

Meg wanted to scold his daddy, but she simply smiled and touched her forehead to Stockton's. "Yeah. But I'm okay."

"Yeah?" He focused on the side of her face she'd fallen on, and she wondered if she had a black eye or a bruise. "Did Daddy kiss it better?"

Eli made a sound like he'd been shot, and he said, "Stockton, come on, bud."

Meg shook her head, her emotions teeming so close to the surface. "No, Stockton. Your daddy didn't kiss it better."

"Should I?"

"Stockton," Eli said again. The child had a knack for tuning his father right out.

The little boy leaned forward and kissed Meg's cheek

and then her forehead, missing the sore spots entirely —thankfully.

She grinned at him. "All better." Meg cut a glance toward Eli and found him staring, his hands hanging loosely at his sides. He looked like someone had stunned him, what with his mouth hanging slightly open.

"It's kind of puffy." Stockton touched her eyebrow, and Meg winced away from his fingertip.

"I'll get her some more ice." Eli left, and Meg settled Stockton into her side.

"What time is it, bud?"

"I don't know."

"Did you eat lunch yet?"

"Celia is making it now." He couldn't say Celia's name properly, so it came out like *Seela*, and Meg stroked his hair.

"What are we going to do for the break? No school or anything."

"Daddy says he's taking me to the movies this afternoon."

Meg had the sudden urge for popcorn. "That sounds great," she said.

Eli walked in as Stockton said, "You should come."

Eli extended the ice bag toward her as he asked, "She should come to what?"

"The movies." Stockton looked up at Eli, but his gaze had locked onto Meg's. In the past, she'd gone on dozens of family outings on her day off. In Bora Bora, they'd gone to museums, beaches, movies, shell-collecting, out on a whale watching safari, and much more. It wasn't abnormal for Stockton to want her to come, and it wasn't unusual for her to go.

But now?

She had no idea what to say. She couldn't tell if Eli didn't want her to come, or he'd just lost his voice again. Was he thinking about Caroline right now?

Meg tore her eyes from his and took the ice, settling it over her puffy eye and cheek. "I don't think I can," she said at the same time Eli said, "She should stay here and rest."

So he didn't want her to come.

Meg's stomach felt like someone had chopped it in half and sewn it back together inside out. She couldn't swallow, and she was about to cry again.

"Come on, bud. Let's leave her alone." Eli held his hand out, a clear indication he wanted Stockton to go with him.

The little boy finally complied, tucking his hand in his father's and letting him pull him off the bed. They held hands as they walked out of the bedroom, with Eli bringing the door gently closed behind him. He didn't look back, and Meg felt like she'd been staked right through the heart.

While she'd wanted to quit when she'd first told Eli about her feelings and he'd hid behind his first wife, she hadn't been able to find anything.

But now...she lowered the ice bag and set it on the

nightstand. Anything would be better than staying in this luxury lodge with the man of her dreams just a wall away —at least physically. But emotionally, he was worlds away, and Meg couldn't keep getting hurt every time they spoke more than ten words to each other.

She got out of bed and over to the desk, the pounding in her head only on her right side, where she'd hit. It radiated from the front of her skull to the back, down to her jawbone and back behind her ear.

But she opened her laptop and started getting the job board tabs open. She could go anywhere, do anything. She had no ties to Coral Canyon, and while she'd only nannied for the past fourteen years, surely she could learn how to scan a gallon of milk and count change.

Anything would be better than subjecting herself to the perfect torture that was being with Eli Whittaker and not being his.

THE NEXT DAY, she still hadn't found anything to pay her bills, though her face was feeling better. Eli had texted earlier that morning that he'd take care of Stockton that day, that she should go ahead and take another twenty-four hours to rest, heal, whatever.

Rest, heal, whatever.

Those were his exact words. It was the *whatever* that

had Meg wondering what to fill her time with. She could only take so many naps, and while she didn't want to be seen with the perfectly round circle under her eye, she didn't want to spend the next day and night cooped up in her room.

The scent of yeast first drew her out of her bedroom to find Celia making bread for that night's family dinner. The following evening, Graham had arranged a Christmas meal for the company, and the next night was Christmas Eve, and Celia would once again make copious amounts of meat, potatoes, breads, desserts and more for the friends and family meal.

Andrew, another of Eli's older brothers, had requested breakfast on Christmas morning, and Laney was making that so Celia could stay home and enjoy the holiday with her family.

Meg loved the family atmosphere at Whiskey Mountain Lodge and her resolve to find another job wavered, just as it had over Thanksgiving.

She went into the kitchen, prepared to say she was fine at least two dozen times. "Need some help?" she asked Celia, who turned and gave her a warm smile. Meg couldn't remember the last time her mother had smiled at her. They spoke four times a year—on Meg's birthday, her mother's birthday, Christmas, and Mother's Day. Meg had been preparing herself for the obligatory Christmas Day call for a week already.

"Oh, just sit down and let me feed you. You're skin and bones."

Meg didn't argue, because it was nice to have someone take care of her for a change. She spent so much time attending to Stockton's every need that she sometimes wondered what it would be like to be the primary concern for someone.

"You didn't come out of your room last night." Celia set a pan on the stove and opened the fridge to retrieve the carton of eggs.

"I...yeah." Her suite came equipped with a television, attached bathroom, and mini-fridge. She didn't have a kitchen, but she could rinse bowls in the bathroom. "I ate cold cereal with cream for dinner."

"Oh." Celia paused, a stricken look on her face. "Eli?"

Meg shook her head when she should've nodded. "That man is perfectly impossible." Celia flew into action, cracking the eggs with a little too much force as if punctuating her frustration with violent cooking.

"Where is he?" Meg asked, glad her voice sounded semi-normal.

"Oh, he's outside somewhere. Horses or something." Celia whisked and threw in a healthy pinch of salt and a splash of milk. She put a pat of butter in the pan and swirled it around. "I had no idea he'd be so stubborn about his own feelings."

"It's fine," Meg said. *I'm fine. It's fine. Everything's fine.*

"You told him how you feel, didn't you?" Celia paused in her prep and peered at Meg. "That's why you've both been bumbling about with stormclouds above your heads."

Meg nodded, a certain measure of misery pulling through her so strongly she felt the air leak from her lungs. "He said he wasn't over Caroline." She lifted one shoulder in a shrug. "What am I supposed to say to that? How can I compete with her?" A woman Meg didn't even know and had never met—couldn't know, couldn't meet.

The front door opened, and laughter spilled into the lodge. "Please don't say anything." Meg already had enough to deal with.

"Of course I won't." Celia poured the eggs into the hot pan as Graham came around the corner with his wife, Laney.

"Is Stockton outside?" Bailey asked, skipping over to Celia.

"He sure is, pumpkin." Celia beamed down at the little girl, Graham's step-daughter.

"Can I go out, Mom?"

Laney heaved a sigh as she sat at the bar. "Sure thing. Stay wherever Stockton is."

"How are you feeling?" Celia asked, scrambling like a pro and producing a plate of eggs for Meg before Laney could answer.

Meg nodded at Graham and Laney, but she couldn't stay in the kitchen with them. Graham smelled too much like Eli, and the two of them so happily in love made Meg's heart shrivel to the size of a raisin.

And seeing Laney's baby bump...Meg swallowed back her jealousy and loss over what she could never have. So she took her plate, thanked Celia, and headed back to her room.

She'd eaten in her room before, and it wasn't like her mother was at the lodge to reprimand her. The very thought of her mom at Whiskey Mountain Lodge sent shivers down her spine.

She ate with something blaring from the TV and she surfed through the available jobs on the boards she'd subscribed to. It wasn't an easy task to search for a new job. She wasn't sure where she wanted to live, if she wanted to keep nannying, or pretty much anything else.

Her phone rang, and Meg stared at the name on it, because no one usually called her. She had very few friends over the age of twelve, and her former employers weren't the type to call and chat.

Mom.

Dread filled Meg's chest, but she answered the call. Her mother would simply redial every ten seconds until Meg picked up.

"Hey, Mom." She infused as much false cheer into her voice as she possibly could. There was plenty of holiday cheer and charm at the lodge, but none of it had seeped into Meg's soul yet.

"Meg, how are you?"

So her mother wanted something. Meg could tell from the first thing her mom said when she called. And asking her how she was meant her mother needed a favor.

"I'm doing great." She didn't tell her about the fall. It wouldn't matter anyway.

"Carrie's kids have come down with the flu."

"Oh, that's too bad." Meg pulled in a breath and held it. Carrie and Brittany were Meg's older sisters, and they were twins who did everything right. They were ten when Meg was born, and she'd never quite fit into a family that had been complete before she'd even shown up.

"Yes, it is."

More silence.

"What's Brittany doing for Christmas?" Meg asked, because she knew what was coming next.

"Oh, she and James are on that cruise with the kids."

"Mm hm." Meg was not going to offer.

"I'm wondering what you're doing at the lodge. Maybe there's room for one more."

Why her mother would want to spend the holidays with her, Meg could not comprehend. Though she supposed she knew exactly what it felt like to be alone, abandoned, unwanted.

She heaved a great big sigh. "Can you drive?"

Her mother had been forty-three when she'd given birth to Meg, and now, thirty-two-years later, Meg was sure she couldn't make the eight-hour drive from Boulder to Coral Canyon.

Her mom laughed, but it wasn't the happy kind. "Of course not. Brittany took my license at Thanksgiving. I swear I didn't see that tractor."

"You hit a tractor?"

"It pulled out right in front of me."

"Mom, tractors are *huge*." Meg wanted to laugh, but she knew she shouldn't.

"Can you come pick me up?" Her mom asked like it was a couple of blocks away, that they got together all the time for ham and mashed potatoes, to exchange gifts and sip hot apple cider.

But the truth was, Meg hadn't spent Christmas with any member of her family in thirteen years. The first year after she'd graduated high school, she'd gone to Florida to visit her father. Since her parents had divorced when she was four, she hardly knew the man, and she could admit now that she'd made the trip specifically to make her mom angry.

And she had.

Since then, she'd spent holidays with her kids and the families she worked for. It was better for everyone that way.

"Well?" her mom asked.

"*Well*, I'll need to talk to my boss. I'll call you back." Meg hung up before her mother could say another word.

She faced the closed bedroom door, wondering if she should just wait ten minutes and then call her mom back and say, "Sorry, he said no."

After all, then she wouldn't have to endure the holidays with her mother nor would she have to talk to Eli.

THREE

ELI ADORED his time spent in the stables. He loved horses, and taking care of them, and talking to them like they were friends. Honestly, besides his brothers, his horses were all he had left.

"I used to talk to Meg," he told a mare the color of butter. He'd named her Caroline, and he spent a lot of time with her, almost like she could replace his wife. Which was ridiculous. Eli knew that, but yet he gravitated toward the light-colored mare everyday before he left the stable.

"But she doesn't like me anymore." He stroked the horse's nose, wondering if what he'd said was true. Probably not. If she truly didn't like him anymore, she wouldn't avoid him so completely.

Marbles wandered over to the fence where Eli leaned and lifted his head over the top rung. "Hey, bud." This horse was gray and white and black, all swirled together like the real marble in the lodge.

The horses didn't talk back, but Eli didn't need them to. They kept him company, and that was what he needed.

He left the stables and walked back up the path to the yard, where Stockton had been making snowmen and forts for days. The wind bit at Eli's cheeks and he hunkered down in his coat. "Stock," he called. "You okay? Warm enough?"

"Yeah." His son could play outdoors for hours, and Eli thanked the Lord again for bringing them back to Wyoming where his son could have the life only this back-country lodge could offer. It sure beat sitting in a hotel room with the TV on.

Bailey came around one of the walls of the fort, and Eli knew his brother had arrived at the lodge. Still, he stayed outside for several minutes, talking to the kids and helping them arrange the snowballs they'd built into a large snowbeast.

He finally went into the house through the back door, the kiss of warmth almost painful against his frozen nose. "Woo boy!" Eli whistled and came around the corner from the mudroom to find Graham Laney and Celia in the kitchen. No Meg. "It is cold out there."

He wasn't sure if he was relieved Meg wasn't with them or disappointed. He'd grown so used to her being *right there*, that it felt odd she wasn't.

"Wishing you were back in Bora Bora now, aren't you?" Graham grinned at his brother.

"Nah." Eli took off his hat and shook the snow from it. "I actually like the snow. Stockton is going crazy. Third snowman this week." Eli grinned, truly happy that his son was enjoying himself so much.

Eli took off his coat and boots and hung them in the mudroom before entering the kitchen and taking a marshmallow treat dipped in caramel. "Celia, I love you."

"That's what all the boys say." She let Eli press a kiss to her cheek before he turned to Laney and Graham.

"How's the baby?" If anyone was as excited as Graham about having another Whittaker, it was Eli. More babies for someone else meant less pressure from his mother. Though she'd advised him last night to follow his heart and it wouldn't lead him astray.

But Eli had no idea what his heart was doing. Or where it was going. Or how he should follow it. Falling in love with Caroline had been easy and instant. He'd never be able to replicate it, and his mom had said he didn't need to.

That at least had lifted a burden from his shoulders. He still didn't know what to do about Meg, so he'd done nothing.

"Doing great." Laney put the last bit of biscuit in her mouth. "Graham was just saying he wanted a boy."

"I was not."

"Well, I have a great name for him if it's a boy." Eli

gave them a playful smirk. "Eli is such a strong name, don't you think?"

Graham shook his head and chuckled. "We're not naming our baby after you."

"Why not?"

"I think Laney would like to name a boy after her dad," Graham said, returning to Laney's side and rubbing his thumb over the back of her hand.

"Or yours," she said, gazing up at him.

Eli watched them as absolute love filled the room. He'd felt like this before, and it hurt so, so much that God had taken Caroline from him so soon. Almost unfair.

He didn't ask why, though. His mom had raised him to walk with faith, and that was what he'd been trying to do. He wasn't perfect at it, but he figured if there was anyone who knew what they were doing, it was the Lord.

Someone entered the kitchen, and Eli turned to find Meg there, the perfect distraction from Graham's bliss. Eli practically jumped toward her, a huge smile on his face. "Hey, Meggy."

She didn't return the smile right away, another oddity in Eli's life he didn't know how to deal with. "What's wrong?" Eli asked.

"It's my mother." She wrung her hands, her dark eyes pools of pure panic. "She called and she's hoping to come here for the holidays."

"It's fine with us," Graham said. "I mean, I don't even live here anymore."

"There's plenty of room," Eli said carefully, wishing Meg would've come to him privately so they could truly talk about the situation. He didn't know everything about Meg, but he knew she and her mother didn't get along well, that Meg *never* went home for the holidays, and that she'd left home a week after she'd graduated from high school.

Meg's gorgeous eyes searched his, and he thought he might be able to fall into them—if he'd let himself. "She doesn't have anywhere else to go, and now that I'm back in the states...."

Eli reached out and ran his hand from Meg's wrist to her shoulder, a quick movement, but probably something he shouldn't have done nonetheless. "Invite her. It'll be fine."

Meg nodded and turned to go back down the hall and Eli spun back to the kitchen, the loss of Meg's presence baffling and disconcerting. His brother wouldn't look at him and Celia stirred something on the stove.

"So what's going on with you two?" Laney asked.

"Nothing," Eli said, but his voice was full of falseness.

"Right," Laney said. "Just like I didn't have a crush on my best friend in high school."

"And look how that turned out." Graham put his arm around his wife's shoulders and grinned at his brother.

"She's my nanny," Eli said. "I'm going to go shower." He left, unwilling to have this conversation with two people who'd already navigated through their hard times.

No, thank you. They had no idea what Eli had been through, and how he felt about Meg was none of their business anyway.

He heard Meg's voice when he arrived in the short hall leading to her room, as she'd left her door open a few inches. He wanted to go talk to her, find out more, but something told him it wasn't a good idea. So he ducked into his suite, locked the door, and did exactly what he'd told Laney and Graham he would: he showered.

WHEN MEG DIDN'T SHOW up for the family dinner, Eli tossed his napkin on his plate and said, "I'll be right back."

Only Andrew looked up from his plate piled with ham, potatoes, and creamed corn. Eli didn't care. Meg should be here. This was the family dinner, and she lived in the lodge.

He knocked on her door, and she opened it a few seconds later. "Oh, Eli." She filled the doorway so he couldn't see past her. "I guess we need to talk. I need tomorrow and the next day off. I know it's the holidays, and Stockton isn't in school, but...I thought maybe you wouldn't be working too much."

She spoke in such a rush, Eli got the feeling he was an ogre of a boss. "It's fine. What are you—is your mom coming?"

She sighed and stepped back, letting the door fall further open to reveal a small carryon open on her bed. "Yeah, I have to go pick her up. It's an eight-hour drive."

"Eight hours?" Alarm filled Eli. "You should fly."

"I don't have the money to fly. And my mom certainly doesn't." She returned to the bed and balled a pair of socks. "And you're not paying for it."

How she could tell he'd just opened his mouth to offer, he didn't know. But he snapped his lips together and then pressed them together as he fumed. She'd never let him pay for more than their negotiated rate. Never took more time off than her two days a week. Never deviated from the schedule.

This must all be very upsetting to her, he thought, sympathy making his heart soft.

"I'll go with you," he offered, unsure of where the words had come from. "It's a long drive to make by yourself. Company will make it easier." He forced himself to stop babbling.

She turned back toward him, disbelief on her face. "You want to drive eight hours to Boulder, Colorado to pick up my surly, ungrateful mom, and then drive eight hours back?"

It actually sounded like a nightmare, but Eli nodded. "Sure, why not?"

Meg looked like she could think of a dozen reasons why not, and honestly most of them were probably on Eli's list too.

"I won't be good company."

"Remember when I didn't get that bid for the wave rider?" He cocked his head at her when finally, *finally* a small smile touched that mouth he'd been dreaming of. "I wasn't good company then, and who wouldn't leave my side?"

"That's because Stockton doesn't deserve to be an orphan," she said without missing a beat. But they were bantering—finally. The playful edge in her eye had returned, and Eli felt more like himself than he had in a month.

"You shouldn't be alone right now either," he said.

"I'll be fine."

He hated that word, and hated it even more when Meg said it. It had taken Eli a year to figure out that when Meg said she was fine, she really wasn't.

"What time are you leaving?"

Meg took a step toward him, abandoning her laundry on the bed. "You're not coming."

"What are you going to drive? *My* truck?"

She paused, her dark eyes practically shooting lasers at him. "May I please borrow your truck?"

"Sure." He grinned. "I'll give you the keys in the morning. What time are you leaving?" Eli knew how to play games and win, and though this thing with Meg was anything but a game, he really wanted to win. He didn't want her driving eight hours across two states in the dead of winter by herself. It was a safety issue.

"Early," she said, driving a knife into his heart.

He groaned as if she'd physically done it. "You know I hate getting up early."

"Then just leave the keys with me now." She held out her hand, palm up, an expectant look on her face. "You can't leave your horses anyway. And what about Stockton?"

Eli's mind started to race. He could take Stockton down to Graham's. He knew he and Laney weren't doing anything but maybe coming up here to hang out. And while Laney was pregnant and technically on bed rest, he could get the name of her hired help and get the man to come take care of the horses for two days. Heck, Eli could afford to pay the man whatever he asked.

"I'll work it out," he said.

"Eli." She deflated, and Eli liked the sound of his name in her voice, but not the frustration that came with it.

"I'm worried about you," he said, finally letting some of his defenses slip too.

"You don't get to worry about me." But the way she looked at him, all hope and need, he thought she could really use someone to care about her.

"I care about you," he said carefully. "What if the weather's bad? What if you get a flat tire?"

"I have a cell phone."

"Meg." He took the few steps to her, closing the distance between them, at least physically. "It'll be fun, like that first road trip we took when I was still trying to decide if I should hire you or not." He gazed down at her, thinking it would be natural to take her into his arms, comfort her, whisper assurances that the holidays wouldn't be ruined with her mother at the lodge, and then kiss her.

His heart roared and raced at the very idea, and the moment between them electrified as it lengthened.

"What made you decide to hire me on that trip?"

"Haven't I ever told you?"

She shook her head, her longer hair brushing her shoulders now. He pushed it back and let his hand trail down her arm again. Why that felt like the most intimate gesture in the world, he wasn't sure.

"You knew where the diapers were in the supermarket," he said. "And I had no idea. I knew then I'd never survive without you."

She smiled, the slow, genuine kind he'd seen before. "So I guess now's not a great time to put in my two weeks notice."

Eli felt like he'd been punched in the gut with a fiery fist. "What?"

Meg backed up, and Eli watched the indecision rage across her fair features. "I'm quitting, Eli. I can't keep doing this."

Eli couldn't get his brain to work. *Doing what?* rang through his ears, but he couldn't get it to come out of his mouth. Meg was irreplaceable, that much he knew. Stockton would be devastated.

Heck, Eli was feeling that devastation right now, rolling through him, over him, around him like a tidal wave had pulled him out into a strong riptide.

"That's your final decision?" he asked.

"I just said it, didn't I?" She kept her back to him as she continued to fold laundry, placing some of it in the suitcase and some in piles on the bed.

"Doesn't sound final."

"I'm leaving at six o'clock in the morning." It sounded like a concluding note to the conversation, almost like she was saying *Goodbye, Eli*.

He turned and headed for the door, his own bag to pack. "See you in the morning." He left, only a few hours to make arrangements for his son and his horses, get his own laundry done, a bag packed, and his thoughts to line up so he could figure out how to talk Meg out of leaving him.

No. He shook his head as he entered his bedroom. Not him. Stockton. He didn't want Meg to abandon *Stockton*.

FOUR

MEG BARELY SLEPT, but she couldn't just leave when she wanted. Eli still had the keys, and if she knew him at all—and she did—he'd be late for their six o'clock departure. He really wasn't a morning person.

So when she crept down the hall and into the foyer, finding Eli on the couch there, his face illuminated by the blue light of his phone, was a bit startling. "You're up?" she asked, thinking maybe she didn't know Eli Whittaker as well as she thought she did.

He jumped to his feet, lowering his phone but only taking a single step before pausing. "I can't see."

A giggle slipped from her lips before Meg could call it back or silence it.

"Ah, my eyes are adjusting. You look great. Can hardly see your black eye at all."

"Very funny." She navigated to the wall where the fireplace was and slid her fingers along the surface until she found the light switch. The foyer flooded with light, which caused Eli to groan and shield his eyes.

"It's way too early for that much light."

"You're welcome to go on back to bed." Meg had wrestled with herself for much of the night. Yes, she wanted him to come. He'd be a great buffer between her and her mother, provide company on the long drive down to Boulder, and maybe she'd get to talk to him about something real as an added bonus.

But at the same time, she absolutely did not want to expose him to her mother for any longer than necessary, and the thought of talking to him sent a truckload of fear right through her. Hadn't she said enough already?

The constant tug of war within her own mind was utterly exhausting.

"Nice try," he said. "I've arranged everything with Stockton and the horses, and I'm all yours for the next two days."

Her eyebrows shot up, and his cheeks turned pink within a single heartbeat. "I mean—"

"I know what you mean," she said, holding out her hand. "Keys, please." Honestly, she'd take Eli for two days if that was all she could get. It was better than nothing. The very fact that she thought so angered her, and she waggled her fingers impatiently.

"I'll drive if you want." He wore those jeans that made her want to look twice, a solid blue button-down shirt with a black leather jacket over that, and his cowboy hat. Oh, and the hint of danger in his eyes, along with a little smirk that said he knew exactly what he was doing.

"Fine. You drive. I don't care." Meg had never spoken to her boss the way she was with Eli. Anyone, actually. She was usually agreeable, fun to be around, and easy-going. But something about Eli just set her every nerve on fire.

She reached for her bag at the same time he lunged for it. "I've got it." His hand brushed hers, and she yanked hers back almost like he'd stung her.

"Sorry," she murmured, though she wasn't sure why she felt the need to apologize.

He kept his eyes fixed on hers and released her bag, straightening inch by inch. His hand touched hers again, and she blinked, her heartbeat fluttering like humming-bird's wings.

"Meg," he whispered. "I've been a complete idiot, and I'm...." His voice trailed into nothing, and his fingers laced through hers. Holding his hand felt like nothing Meg had ever experienced before, and she never wanted to let go.

His skin was warm, rough along the edges of his fingers where he worked with ropes and saddles and horse-shoes. The world swayed, the scent of Eli's cologne so intoxicating, and the heat in the lodge entirely too warm.

She hadn't realized she'd let her eyes drift closed until Eli tugged her closer, right into his arms. Her eyes popped open as she realized where she stood, then settled closed again as she listened to the thrumming of his heart beneath his shirt.

She had so much to say, and nothing at the same time. Eli hadn't finished his sentence and didn't seem to be in any hurry to do so. Humming sounded from somewhere, and then footsteps followed, and Eli jumped back from Meg as Andrew reached the top of the stairs and turned on the light in the hall.

Meg hadn't had time to even process what had just happened, let alone tell her muscles to back up.

"Oh, hey you two." Andrew sized them up, keen interest in his expression. "Headed to Colorado?"

"Yeah." Eli flashed an easy smile. Everything with him always came so easily, and Meg had always marveled at it. Now, it simply annoyed her.

"If he'll ever give up the keys," Meg said.

Eli laughed and picked up their bags. "I'm driving. So let's go already. I can't believe we haven't left yet." He gave her that trademark smirk and stepped toward the front door. Meg rolled her eyes but made to follow Eli.

As she stepped out into the cold, she wondered what in the world she was doing. Eight hours trapped in a car with Eli? She already felt slightly insane from whatever had just happened in the foyer.

"Seriously," she muttered under her breath, a great white cloud puffing out before her as the motion lights kicked on. "What is happening?"

Eli set the bags down behind his four-door truck and

dug in his pocket for the keys. "We're going on a road trip." He beamed back at her as if she'd asked him a serious question.

She watched and waited while he loaded their luggage. Then Meg cocked her hip and folded her arms. "Eli, I think this is a mistake."

"Why?"

Meg threw her hands up in frustration. "Because...." She glared at him, her emotions rioting just beneath the surface of her skin, just behind her tongue. "Because I like you so much, and you used your wife as the reason we couldn't be together, or even *try* to be together."

Her chest felt so tight, so tight. She shook her head, her thoughts colliding with one another. "And I may not have gone to college, but I can see you like me too. I'm not stupid."

Eli stood there, glorious and beautiful in the winter atmosphere, his broad shoulders and tall stature almost imposing.

"So I think I should just go alone." Meg swiped angrily at her eyes. Would she never stop crying?

"I don't think you're stupid," Eli said, his voice this freaky calm tone that only made Meg angrier.

She scoffed and glared at him. "Okay." She'd taken two steps to round the truck and get in when he added, "I do like you."

Her feet froze as if someone had poured water on them, and in these December temperatures, it had solidified upon contact. "Let's just go." She could see he wasn't going to give her the keys and go back to bed. She went around the truck and got in the passenger side.

Eli climbed behind the wheel. "I made a mistake," he said. "Do you think you could give me another chance?"

She'd give him a hundred chances, but she kept her arms folded across her chest and her gaze out her window, afraid to hope. Afraid to get her heart stomped on again by this man. Afraid to spend the next eight hours with him, no matter what beautiful things he said.

"I'm sorry," he said next, and Meg's anger softened with those two simple words. He put the truck in gear and backed up before getting them on the road. "I made a mistake at Thanksgiving. I know that. I just don't know how to fix it."

Meg didn't know either. But they had eight hours to figure it out, and she prayed God would help her know when to listen, what to say, and how to feel.

NEITHER OF THEM said much in the first hour. But once they hit Jackson Hole, Eli asked if she wanted breakfast, and they stopped at a busy diner. It was loud, vibrant, and some of the tension leaked from Meg as she ate pancakes, bacon, and fried potatoes. She drank entirely too much coffee, and she told Eli they'd have to stop so she could go to the bathroom often.

"Anytime," he said as they loaded up again.

"Have you always been this agreeable?"

"I'm sure my wife wouldn't say so," he said. "Or my brothers."

Meg watched him while he buckled his seatbelt and put the truck in gear as if he hadn't just opened the floodgate by mentioning his wife. "Tell me about her," she said. For all she knew about Eli, she didn't know much about Caroline.

"Who? Caroline?"

"Yes, Caroline. I know you named a horse after her."

"Yes, I did." His knuckles flexed on the steering wheel and he swallowed. "She was a health nut," he said. "Always making whole wheat tortillas from scratch and putting bean sprouts on everything. Even peanut butter sandwiches." He chuckled, his low voice hearty and throaty at the same time.

Meg relaxed in the seat, this kind of conversation meaningful and somewhat enjoyable. "You don't even like peanut butter."

"But Caroline did." Eli shrugged one shoulder and merged onto the highway leading south.

"So you just pretended?"

"No, of course not. When she made peanut butter sandwiches, I ate something else."

"She was...serious about some things, and laid back about others. She loved the ocean." Eli's voice took on a faraway quality as he continued. "She was the reason I took the job in Bora Bora. I thought she would've loved it there."

"I'm sure she would've," Meg said, her voice full of kindness. Listening to him talk about Caroline with such reverence made Meg realize how much he'd loved his wife. To think she had any chance with him at all was ludicrous.

Thankfully, he fell silent, obviously lost in his warm, wonderful memories of his wife. Misery filled Meg, and she thought she should've just let Eli pay for the airplane tickets she needed.

Help me, she thought, the only prayer she could string together.

"Okay, your turn," he said.

"My turn for what?"

"Tell me something about you I don't know."

A couple of things sprang into her mind, but she bit them back. "You know everything about me."

"Oh, I'm sure that's not true." He glanced at her and then put his focus back on the road.

Meg couldn't vocalize how unwanted she felt. Couldn't tell him about her teenage health issues, or how she'd once sworn she'd never get married. Of course, if she wanted a real relationship with him, she'd have to tell him at some point, but not on this trip. Not so soon.

"It is," she said instead of telling him anything personal. "Okay, maybe you don't know that I strongly dislike cottage cheese."

He chuckled again. "See? I didn't know that." He smiled at her and reached out his hand as if he'd hold hers.

She stared at it, then lifted her eyes to Eli's handsome face. That strong, bearded jaw, those full lips, the long, straight nose that made his face full of perfect lines and angles. His light brown hair curled out from under his cowboy hat, and she wanted to twirl the locks around her fingers just before she kissed him.

He let his hand drop to his lap in the same moment Meg decided to unbuckle her seat belt and slide across the seat to sit right next to him. She tucked her arm under his and he curled his fingers around hers as she leaned into him.

"This is crazy, right?" she whispered, the sound of her voice barely louder than the radio.

"Probably," he said in the same hushed tone. "But it feels...good."

Meg smiled to herself, Eli's eye catching hers in the rear-view mirror. He started laughing, and Meg couldn't help herself as she joined in. Thirty minutes later, two hours into their trip, she was just starting to doze off when he said, "We should've flown."

"Oh, you're not enjoying yourself?"

"I am." He squeezed her hand. "It's just—six more hours." He exhaled, and Meg closed her eyes again.

"Tell me some of those stories you tell Stockton," she said. "They'll pass the time, and we'll be in Boulder before you know it."

"What stories do I tell Stockton?"

"About what you and your brothers used to do growing up. Skiing. Stealing peas from the Cullets. That kind of stuff."

"Oh, you want childhood memories."

"Mm."

"If I share, you'll have to."

"Don't worry," she said. "You'll meet my mother in a few hours and you'll know everything about my childhood." If only the thought didn't strike so much fear in her bloodstream.

"All right then. There was this one time Graham dared me and Andrew to jump our family van over the canal...."

FIVE

ELI STOPPED TALKING the moment Meg's breathing evened. She slept against his side, her head nestled into his bicep, and it felt so good. So, so good. He couldn't even describe the feelings flowing through him, only that he really enjoyed whatever they were.

"Thank you, Lord." He felt...content, maybe for the first time since Caroline had died. The miles rolled by with Meg slumbering and Eli making mental lists about why he could or couldn't have a relationship with his nanny.

An hour passed before his phone rang, which caused Meg to groan as it interrupted her sleep. The truck's electronic voice cut into the low music with, "Call from Stockton."

"Hey, sorry," Eli said, moving his arm so he could connect the call through the truck's Bluetooth technology.

"Hey, bud," he answered. "Are you helping Celia with breakfast?"

"Daddy, it's almost lunch time."

Eli checked the clock and found it barely past ten, so that wasn't true. He didn't argue the point though, just laughed and said, "So you must've gotten up early."

"Celia said I can have a second breakfast, so she's making cinnamon toast right now."

Second breakfast. Eli had noticed his son growing out of his clothes too, so the boy must be having a major growth spurt. "That's great, Stock. One of your favorites."

"Where are you guys?"

"Somewhere in Wyoming," Eli said as Meg glanced around. But the landscape in southern Wymoing was all the same. Flat road stretching forever, with snow piled on both sides. Eventually, Cheyenne would appear, and Eli thought they'd stop there for lunch.

"Graham said he's going to take me to town today to see Grandma."

"That's awesome." Eli had specifically asked his brother to take Stockton to see their mom, who wanted to take her grandson shopping for Christmas to get gifts for the family. Eli had said she didn't need to do that, that he could take his own kid to the dollar store to pick out something for his uncles and everyone else he wanted to.

But he hadn't had time. Or had he and he simply hadn't done it? The past month felt like it had been wiped out of his memory completely. Like he'd been in a trance and was just now coming out of it.

"And then Annie said I can help her make sure all the beds are ready for Christmas Eve."

"Also great," Eli said. Graham took care of the family celebrations, even though he didn't live at the lodge anymore. So Eli wasn't exactly sure why they needed beds to be ready. Perhaps everyone was planning to come sleep over on Christmas Eve. He knew his mom and Beau would for sure.

"So after you do those things, you'll remember what I asked you to do, right?" Eli could practically hear his son's mind churning as he tried to remember what he was supposed to do.

"Oh! With the horse."

"That's right. With the horse." Eli had asked Stockton to draw a card for Laney and Graham, because Eli had bought a new horse for their ranch as a Christmas gift. "And what did you decide to name her? That should be on the card too."

"I was thinking of making a box," Stockton said. "My art teacher showed us how to fold these papers and stuff."

"Sure. Whatever. We just want to have something to give them inside." The horse would be delivered by Christmas, but Eli couldn't put it under the tree. "Are you going to surprise me with the name?"

Meg caught his eye, and Eli waved to indicate he'd tell her about it in a minute. She combed her fingers through her hair, and Eli wished she'd kept it in the stylish A-line she'd had since the day he'd met her. This long look just didn't suit her, in his opinion. But he knew enough not to express such an opinion to a woman.

"I'm still deciding," Stockton said, the last word getting all twisted on his tongue.

Eli laughed. "All right. Well, call me when you decide."

"Meggy's not here to help me, so I don't know."

Eli met Meg's eye again, but she looked away quickly. He wanted to tell her she simply couldn't quit, that Stockton would fall apart without her. He swallowed, unsure if he should use his son to get what *he* wanted—to keep Meg in both of their lives.

"The toast is ready." Which was six-year-old code for good-bye. Eli said he'd talk to Stockton later, and they hung up. He exhaled, glad he had friends and family that were so willing to take his son when Eli couldn't be there.

He glanced at Meg again, and she'd folded her arms and gone back to staring out her window. "How close are we to Cheyenne?" she asked, turning toward him.

"About forty-five minutes."

"Do you want to stop for lunch?"

"I sure do." He wished she'd slide back across the seat and hold his hand as possessively as she had earlier. It felt nice to be wanted again, to feel like he meant something to someone besides a little boy who'd already lost so much.

"I bought Graham and Laney a new horse for their

ranch," he said instead of asking her to return to his side. "Stockton's gonna name it and make them a card."

"Or a box."

"Right. Or a box."

Silence fell between them again, and Eli couldn't stand it. "He'll be heart-broken when you leave."

That got her to face him, her expression a perfect storm of emotions he couldn't sort through fast enough. "He's resilient."

"That's your answer?"

Meg shrugged. "I have no idea what's going on."

"Slide back over here and hold my hand. I liked that." Eli kept his eyes on her longer than normal, but the traffic on this lonely stretch of highway was non-existent.

She pressed her lips together, and said, "I'd like to get my hair cut in Cheyenne. We'll have time, don't you think?"

Surprise cut through what else he'd been planning to say. "You want to get a haircut?"

"My mom won't like this one. It'll be one less thing she can nag me about."

Eli let a few seconds go by while he thought about what she'd said. "Your mom nags you about a lot of things?"

"Everything," Meg said. "It's no wonder my dad left when he did."

"How old were you?"

"Four."

"And you have two older sisters, right?"

"Twins, yes. They're a decade older than me." She turned back to the window, her voice falling in pitch and volume as she said, "I've never fit in my family, not even for a single day."

Eli's whole chest wailed, his heart beating furiously fast at the agony in her tone. "I'm sure that's not true."

"Oh, it's true."

He really wanted her beside him now, so he could whisper comforting things to her and assure her that he wanted her, that she fit with him.

Before he could organize his words so they didn't sound blunt or creepy, she said, "I fit with kids. They've always liked me, and I've always liked them."

"You're a great nanny." He liked this conversation. Sure, he knew things about Meg, like how she took her coffee, and what kind of eggs she liked. He could pick from any menu what she'd order and be right nine times out of ten.

The sort of things he knew about her came from their casual acquaintance and the sheer amount of time they'd spent together over the past four years. But he didn't know much about her family, and she'd never told him such emotional things before.

She sniffed, and Eli found her wiping her eyes when he looked at her. "What's wrong?"

"Nothing."

But it was obviously something. He had no idea what

to do. Caroline had cried several times over the course of their four-year marriage, but Eli had been able to take her into his arms, tell her all the reassurances in the world, and kiss everything better.

But he couldn't do any of that with Meg. In fact, if he did, he felt sure he'd only make things worse.

"What do you want for lunch?" he asked, hoping to get her talking about something lighter, something less important.

"There's a great Mexican place in Cheyenne," she said. "Laney said she'd text me the name of it." She pulled out her phone and started tapping. "She went to college in Cheyenne."

"Right." Eli didn't keep track of details like that, but Meg did. Meg excelled at details, and when she finished texting, he said, "You sure you don't want to come hold my hand again?"

She turned toward him fully, actually adjusting in her seat to do so. "I need to know what your intentions are first."

"My intentions?" His fingers tightened on the steering wheel.

"Like, are you just doing this because you don't want me to quit?"

Horror shot through Eli, making his blood feel like ice in his veins. "No," he said with as much force as possible. "Of course not." She'd said she could tell he liked her. And now she didn't believe him?

He'd messed up so badly with her, and a dose of helplessness dove through him. "It's like you said. It's obvious I like you." Even Graham had asked him about it. Laney too.

She slid toward him, but before she touched him, she said, "My two weeks notice still stands."

Eli tucked her hand inside his and lifted it to his lips. After a quick kiss on the back of her hand, he said, "Well, I'll have to do my best to talk you out of that over the next fourteen days."

She simply cocked one eyebrow and settled their hands on her knee. "You can try."

Oh, he'd try. And while Eli had experienced some failures in his life, he felt certain this wasn't going to be one of them.

THREE HOURS LATER, they'd arrived in Cheyene, eaten at Taco Jose's, and Meg had just texted to say she'd be done with her hair in five minutes. Eli had opted to stay in the truck while she went into the salon, and he'd taken an hour-long nap since he'd risen at five o'clock that morning. He rarely got up before eight AM, so the loss of three hours of sleep was significant.

Sure enough, only five minutes passed before Meg pushed out of the salon, her A-line crisp and clean and so, so cute.

He got out of the truck, the smile on his face almost ridiculous. "Hey there, pretty lady." It felt almost natural to talk to her in such a flirty tone, to sweep his arm around her waist and pull her close.

She didn't protest when he did that, but then time stalled as she looked up at him and he gazed down at her. It felt like a moment where a boyfriend would kiss his girlfriend, tell her how amazing her hair looked, and ask her if she was ready to hit the road again.

His eyes drifted to her mouth, wondering—not for the first time—what she'd taste like. His pulse went nuts, and his mind blanked.

After a breath or two, she pushed against his chest and said, "We better get going. We're still a few hours away."

He fell back several steps, the loss of her body next to his tearing through him. It had been too long since he'd dated, because he'd never frozen like that before. Eli had always known what he wanted—and how to get it. He'd met Caroline while he'd worked at a resort in California. She was the concierge and he was the events manager, and they'd had to participate in a lot of meetings and joint ventures.

Their spark had been instant and hot, and she'd actually asked him to dinner before the room had cleared. They'd dated for a year and gotten married on the beach where they both worked. Things had seemed so perfect—until the accident that took her life. Eli hadn't returned to California since.

"Are you coming?"

He turned to find Meg standing at the passenger door. He practically tripped over his own feet to join her. "Your hair looks awesome," he said. "I like this cut on you."

She grinned at him as he opened the door for her. "Thank you."

He went around the front of the truck, careful to avoid the icy patch on the sidewalk, and got behind the wheel. "Anything we need before we get going again?"

"I don't think so. Did you want me to drive?"

"I'm good. I slept for most of the time you were in the salon."

Meg set her jaw and said, "Let's do this then. The sooner we get there, the sooner we can get back to Coral Canyon."

SIX

MEG FELT five seconds away from crying and they were still on the outskirts of Boulder. She'd felt like this for the past half an hour, and they still had twenty minutes of winding through the city until they pulled up to her mother's house.

That time seemed to pass in a single breath, because before she knew it, Eli put the truck in park and said, "You ready?"

Meg shook her head, taking in the snow-covered walkways, the way the rain gutters dipped, and how dingy the windows looked.

The curtains fluttered, and Meg knew her time was short. *Please help me endure this holiday*, she prayed before turning to Eli. "I guess we better go in before she comes out."

Eli kept his eyes on the house too. "She doesn't get out much, does she?"

"No." Meg thought that was one reason her mom was so mean. She'd simply forgotten how to interact with other people, though a small voice whispered in the back of Meg's mind that her mom had always been surly, even before she retired.

"All right then, let's—"

"Eli, she's really mean."

He finally turned his attention to her, and Meg's anxieties spilled out of the box she'd been carefully keeping them in.

"I've worked with plenty of mean people."

Meg shook her head again. "No, Eli. You've dealt with people in a bad mood. Someone who wanted a refund or thought your event was poorly planned. This is way beyond that." The opening of the front door caught her attention and drew it away from Eli. "She is like nothing you've ever encountered."

He didn't argue with her or try to say she was exaggerating, which Meg really appreciated. "All right. Do we need a code word?" They often worked out code words when going into stressful situations, usually with Stockton. That way, she could say, "I really don't like artichokes," and he would know she wanted to leave whatever party they'd gone to.

"We're taking her back to the lodge with us," she said. "There's no getting away from her."

Eli wore a pained expression, almost like he was trying to make a difficult decision and couldn't. "We can do this," he finally said. "*You* can do this."

"She's waiting." She nodded toward the front door, her heart sinking all the way to the soles of her feet. "Might as well get this over with." Meg exhaled and opened her door. Eli met her at the front of the truck and took her hand before she could warn him not to touch her. After all, her mother was very traditional and she wouldn't like—

"Meg," her mom called. "Who did you bring with you?"

Meg almost shoved Eli away from her. "This is my boss, Eli Whittaker," she said as she tromped through the snow that went halfway up her calf. "You look great, Mom."

Her mom's hair had once been dark like Meg's, but it now hung in white strings around her face. She usually had it pulled back into a severe bun, but it didn't look like she'd even gotten around to showering yet today.

She still wore her house robe and the rattiest pair of slippers Meg had ever set eyes on. At least she knew what to get her mother for Christmas now.

"You hold hands with your boss?" Her mom's dark eyes cut right into Meg and then sliced right through Eli. Her gaze raked from his cowboy hat to his feet and back. "I guess he's handsome enough."

As if that was the most important requirement in a boyfriend. Or a boss. Or whatever Eli was. Meg wasn't entirely sure what was going on between her and Eli, how to classify it, or if she'd really quit in two weeks' time.

"Can we come in?" Meg wasn't going to try to get up the four steps with all the snow if her mom wasn't going to invite her in. From the sweet stench of garbage wafting from the house, Meg didn't really *want* to go in. But it would be better than standing out in the arctic temperatures.

"Yes, come in, come in. I can't be heating the whole world." She turned and ambled back inside, the hip she'd broken a decade ago causing a limp on the right side.

Meg exchanged a glance with Eli and mouthed, "I'm sorry," before mounting the steps and entering the house. The living room looked like her mom had started living in it permanently, with blankets piled on the couch and a dirty plate on the side table. But the real smell came from the kitchen, where it was obvious her mother hadn't taken the garbage out in months.

"Mom." Meg glanced around, suddenly knowing what she'd spend the night doing.

"Oh, don't 'Mom' me. I'm doin' fine."

Eli picked up two bags of trash and said, "I'll lend a hand."

"I don't need a hand."

"Mom." Meg put herself between Eli and her mother. "Let him help you. Are you packed? We're leaving very early in the morning."

"Oh, I haven't thought about it."

"Mom, you called me to come get you, remember?"

Her mom opened the fridge and pulled out a can of diet cola. "I'll be ready." Her hawk eyes went to Eli when he banged the door against the wall. "Be careful, boy. This is an old house."

Eli paused, shock making his eyes widen. "I'm thirty-five-years-old, ma'am. I am not a boy."

Meg sucked in a breath, horrified at what he'd said—and how her mother would react. Her mom sputtered, and Eli tipped his cowboy hat and continued into the garage. The fresh air that came in, though it was cold, was a relief.

Meg turned back to her mom and asked, "Can I help you pack?" in the sweetest voice she could muster.

"YOU'RE LEAVING?" Meg couldn't help the slight hint of hysteria in her voice. Her mother had gone to bed an hour ago, but seeing as how she slept in the recliner in the living room and Meg was having this hushed conversation in the kitchen, there wasn't much privacy.

"This is a two-bedroom house," Eli whispered back. "Where do you think I'll sleep?"

Desperation raged through Meg and she pushed her hand through her hair, still not used to the shorter cut. "She refuses to pack," she hissed. "I can't deal with this."

Eli put both hands on her shoulders, grounding her and forcing her to face him. "Meg, sweetheart. Of course you can do this. You're a strong woman, and I believe in you."

She nodded, but only because her neck seemed to have developed a mind of its own, not because she believed him. He got to leave, and the strong surge of jealousy had muted her. That, and the way her mom snuffled and the recliner squeaked as she moved.

Meg pressed her eyes closed, and Eli dropped his hands. "I'll be back bright and early. You'll be okay. Okay?"

Meg was very tired of feeling weak. So she opened her eyes, drew in a deep breath, and nodded. "Okay."

Eli nodded a single time and crept out the garage door. With the garbage gone, and after Meg had emptied almost the entire can of air freshener she'd found under the kitchen sink, the house smelled much better.

Meg winced with the click of the door, the sound almost like a gunshot in her soul. But she was a strong woman, and she *could* do this. She went down the hall to her mother's room and found two baskets of clean laundry. At least her mom had gotten that far.

She tucked her long side pieces of hair behind her ears and opened her mom's closet to find a suitcase. She'd only be staying a couple of days, so she wouldn't need much. Meg lost herself in the monotony of folding laundry, repeating the same motions over and over and getting something measurable done.

Her muscles, bones, and brain begged her to stop, to go

to sleep, but she kept up the work until she'd gotten through all the clothes and packed what she thought her mom would like best. She hadn't gotten along well with her mother in decades, and yet, she still felt this strange connection to her she could only attribute to blood.

Her mind settled with the mindless work, and her thoughts quieted. Finally. She'd been so discombobulated since Thanksgiving, since Eli started holding her hand, since he'd confessed he liked her.

And yet, her mind whispered that he wasn't being genuine. That he hadn't admitted anything until she'd told him she was quitting.

She tried to push those thoughts away, ignore the traitorous feelings. With her mom packed and ready, Meg finally retreated to the bedroom where she'd grown up and climbed into the stale sheets.

Morning came quickly, and a text from Eli sat on her phone that was ten minutes old.

In the driveway with backup.

She hoped that meant hot coffee and fresh pastries. *Getting in the shower now. Give me twenty minutes?*

Your wish is my command.

Meg shook her head and smiled at the text. She'd been saying that to Stockton for years, and Eli had picked up on it and started saying it a year or two ago. Meg had entertained several fantasies of him saying it to her as he held her close, and she smiled up at him coyly, and said, "I wish you'd kiss me."

And he always granted her wish, and it was always the best kiss of her life. Not that she'd had many kisses to begin with, so she didn't have much to go on as far as the fantasies went. But she was almost afraid to kiss Eli for fear that the real thing wouldn't be as good as what she'd conjured up in her mind.

Once she was showered, dressed, and ready for the day, things livened up. Her mother had awakened, and Eli came in, and after consuming an apple fritter and the world's best cup of coffee—it said so right on the to-go cup—Eli started loading up their bags, all smiles and sunshine.

He'd obviously slept better than she had, and Meg let him handle her mom as she didn't seem to know how. Her mother didn't say anything cruel either, which was a miracle all its own.

Eli acted as a buffer between Meg and her mom on the long drive back to the lodge, though her mom sat in the middle seat between them. She didn't say a whole lot, other than to criticize Meg's haircut, to which Eli piped right up and said, "I think it's very flattering." He acted like nothing ever bothered him, but Meg saw the twitch of his jaw and the flash of fire in his eyes before he turned them back to the highway. "And Meg likes it, so that's really what matters."

Her mother didn't seem to know how to deal with someone who disagreed with her or didn't get flustered when she said something they didn't like. Meg wished she was like Eli, but everything her mom said and did annoyed her.

She'd once asked Carrie how she could stand being around their mom so much, as Carrie usually hosted holidays and events at her house in Fort Collins. Her older sister had blinked at her and said, "I don't know what you mean."

So once again, Meg had been the odd man out, the black sheep, the female that didn't fit in the Palmer family. Bora Bora had provided a fantastic excuse for skipping birthday parties, Easter egg hunts, and summer camping trips.

Wyoming wasn't nearly as far away, but surely she couldn't be expected to jaunt the ten hours to Carrie's just to get a few pieces of chocolate in a plastic egg.

By the time Eli pulled into the parking lot at the lodge, dusk had started to settle over the land. He helped her mom navigate the steps and warmth and firelight greeted them all inside the lodge, along with Christmas music and chatter.

It seemed everyone had spent the day together, and all the Whittaker brothers got along so well. Several chairs had been brought out of the dining room and into the foyer, which already held two long couches and a few armchairs.

Eli's mother, Amanda, jumped up from one of the recliners near the fireplace and said, "Eli's back." She hugged her son and gave Meg the kind of motherly smile she'd always longed for. "How was the drive, Meggy?"

"Long." Meg melted into the other woman's embrace, almost wanting to step back and say to her mom, "See? This is how it's done."

Amanda released her and put the brightest, biggest smile on her face. "And you must be Janice. We're so glad you could join us for the holidays this year." She hugged Meg's mom too, who wore a look of genuine surprise on her face.

When she stepped back, she patted her hair and said, "Oh, well, thank you." She gazed around the lodge like she'd never seen anything like it, and Meg supposed that might be true. Whiskey Mountain Lodge was one-of-a-kind, and completely remodeled from top to bottom due to a fire a few years ago.

Whoever had renovated it had invested in the best materials money could buy, and it felt high-end and homey at the same time, with personal touches of artwork and tea lights, paired with the comfortable furniture, marble floors and columns, and dark, shiny wood on the staircase.

Eli and Andrew had been working together this past year to bring more tourists and locals to the lodge, and they used the upper six bedrooms on the third floor for accommodations.

Meg's heart stopped as if someone had shot her with an arrow. She leaned into Eli and asked, "Where's my mother staying?" just as Graham came out of the kitchen with a glass of sparkling apple cider in his hand. The tree lighting would happen any moment, as Eli had told her they were simply waiting for him and Meg to return before they did it and then served dinner.

Eli met her eye, concern in his. "I hadn't thought about it."

"Welcome, everyone," Graham said. "It's so good to have so many friends and family here with us at the lodge this year." He glanced around, the fondness in his expression easy to find. "We'll do the tree lighting first, and this year, we've got our very own Lady of the Manor to do it." He beamed at his mother as she navigated through the crowd to Graham's side. "After that, we'll do our Christmas Eve gifts before we move into the dining room for dinner. The kids have been very hard at work on the name plates and place settings, so be sure to find yours and take it home with you if you want."

As Meg looked around, she realized the only people there were the Whittaker family members, Celia, Bree—who'd decorated the huge Christmas tree—and then Meg and her mother. It felt like a large group, yet also intimate at the same time.

"Oh, and before Mom plugs in the tree, I've been told to warn everyone about the mistletoe. It's been roving, and it doesn't accept excuses." His eyes twinkled as if he himself were Santa Claus, and Meg might have imagined it, but Graham's gaze seemed to linger on her and Eli—still standing very close to one another—before saying, "All right, Mom. Light us up."

Amanda grinned at the group and ducked behind the tree, jostling some of the lower branches and ornaments until she got the plug in the outlet. The tree burst to life in an array of colorful lights, and everyone said, "Ahhh," in tandem, Meg included.

The spirit here was just too strong to ignore, and Meg loved Christmas. So her mother was here. Eli seemed to have a way with her, and Meg thought that maybe, just maybe, her holidays wouldn't be ruined.

SEVEN

ELI BASKED in the magic of the Christmas tree, happiness filling him from his boots to the top of his skull.

He slipped his fingers along Meg's, finally latching on and holding her hand behind their bodies. He squeezed once, leaned down, and said, "I can move Stockton in with me, so your mom doesn't have to go up and down stairs."

"Yeah, that's probably a good idea." She didn't look at him, probably because his mother had zeroed in on them and seemed to know they'd been sharing personal things and holding hands.

"My mother," he muttered as she started across the room toward them.

Thankfully, Stockton got to them first. "Daddy!" The boy flung himself into Eli's arms, and Eli laughed as he dropped Meg's hand and caught his son.

"Hey, bud." He grinned down at him. "Were you good for everyone?"

"Of course he was," Meg said. "Weren't you, Stockton?" She wore a look of such love, Eli wondered how she thought she could quit in twelve days and leave the boy behind.

"Meggy." Stockton squirmed from Eli to Meg, who took him into a hug. "I can't wait to show you the horses. Uncle Graham helped me in the stable yesterday, and we put up new chalk boards."

"That was a secret," Graham said as he arrived. "How are you, Eli? Good drive?" He clapped Eli on the shoulder and they exchanged a quick hug.

"Good enough." The truth was, Eli was exhausted. He'd slept little at the hotel, and his senses had been on such high alert for the entire drive so he could protect Meg from anything her mother might say.

"Janice." Eli's mother arrived on the scene, and Eli had the feeling that he needed to get out of this foyer. "We have something for you." She held out a small, box-shaped package while Meg's mom blinked at it.

"Go on, Mom," Meg murmured, nudging her mother out from behind her. "Take it."

"What is it?" Janice demanded, and Eli had to work hard to keep himself from rolling his eyes.

His mother didn't miss a beat. "Open it and find out."

Meg finally took the package when her mother

continued standing there. "Thank you, Amanda. I think my mom is just tired."

"I'm not tired." She practically ripped the package from Meg's hands and tore into the red and white snowflaked paper. A shoebox emerged, and it held a pair of slippers that were far superior to the threadbare ones she'd been wearing yesterday.

Eli stared at the gift, wondering how his mother had known to get them for her.

"I texted her," Meg whispered as if she'd read Eli's mind. He wanted to slip his arm around her waist and pull her close. The action almost seemed like it would be completely natural, but he didn't do it.

Meg set Stockton on his feet and bent toward him. "Go get our presents, okay, bud?" The little boy scampered off and Eli caught the look of love on Meg's face. It didn't entirely fade when she faced him, and that sent fear right through Eli's heart.

Fear—and hope.

"Those are nice, Mom." Meg smiled at her mother, her normally pretty face absolutely radiant.

Her mom looked up from the shoebox, and for a few terrible moments Eli thought she'd snap at Meg, his mother, everyone. Something dark and dangerous crossed Janice's face, and then she looked at Eli's mom and said, "These *are* nice. Thank you." She drew in a breath. "I don't have anything for anyone." She turned her dark eyes on Meg and a measure of cruelty entered her gaze. "No one told me about gifts."

"It's fine, Mom," Meg said at the same time Eli said, "No one expects you to have gifts. There's usually only one per person, so we're not all exchanging them."

Stockton skipped up to them and said, "This one's for you, Daddy." He handed Eli a soft package that looked like Stock himself had wrapped it, which he probably had.

"Thanks, bud. And Meggy?"

"Right here." He handed Meg a small box that looked like it held jewelry. Eli watched her out of the corner of his eye while he pulled the paper off his present.

"Oh, look, a Hawaiian shirt." Eli grinned at the bright blue fabric with equally neon palm trees and pineapples on it. He held it up to his body. "I do miss the tropical weather."

Meg smiled at him and pulled the end of the white ribbon winding around her box. She picked at the paper, and Laney came over to stand beside Graham before she got it off and the box open.

Meg sucked in a breath and glanced up at Eli. "You did this?"

He peered at the necklace with a few colored gems hanging from the chain, along with a silver M. "I had no idea."

"I did," Laney said. "That blue one's your birthstone." She pointed to the white one. "That one's Stockton's. And that pink one is just because I liked it and it needed three jewels."

Meg looked back at the box and reverently took the necklace out of the box. Eli caught the glassiness of tears in her eyes as Laney helped her put the jewelry on. "Thank you, Laney. I love it."

"Stockton's not your boy," her mom said, and Eli took a half-step in front of Meg and Stockton.

"Graham," he said.

"Let's go see if Celia will let us have any of that chocolate pie." Graham scooped Stockton into his arms amidst a squeal of delight from the little boy and left before he could hear anything he didn't need to.

"Mom."

"You can't even have kids." She scoffed and shuttled a few steps away, clutching her slippers tight. "What kind of woman is that? One who can't have kids. What a waste." She shook her head like she really pitied Meg, but Eli didn't get that sense at all.

Meg made a noise like a leaky balloon, the tears splashing down her face now. She didn't bother to hide them as she met Eli's eyes with absolute terror and desperation in hers. Ever the polite, perfect Meg, she said, "Excuse me," before hurrying out of the foyer and down the hall that led to her bedroom.

Helplessness filled Eli, only driven out by the pure rage he felt for Meg's mother. All the eyes on him felt like lead bricks, and he could only look at one person—his mother.

"Mom, I—thank you for getting the slippers for Janice. I'm going to go get her settled in her bedroom and I'll join everyone for dinner."

"What about Meg?"

"I'll see if she'll come out."

You can't even have kids.

What a waste.

The words tortured him as he led Janice down the same hall where Meg had just escaped and put her bag in Stockton's room. "Meg's right there," he said, indicating the door in the corner. "And Stock and I are across the hall."

Janice said nothing but looked around the room as if she found it absolutely lacking. Eli didn't stay to hear her assessment of it, but simply said, "I'll let you freshen up for dinner. I'll come get you when it's time." He backed out of the room and brought the door closed. He wanted to lock it from the outside, but it didn't have that feature.

He turned toward Meg's bedroom door, his heart struggling to beat against those damaging words her mother had spoken, the feelings he had surging through him. He really liked Meg, and he didn't want her to quit, and he thought maybe he should tell her so in exactly those words.

Before he lost his nerve, he stepped toward the door and knocked on it.

"No," Meg said from inside, and Eli tried the doorknob to find it locked.

"Meg, please let me in." Eli leaned his forehead against the wood, willing to have this conversation through the door if he had to. He didn't really want to, because he had a feeling his mother loitered just around the corner, listening.

"I...I can't, Eli."

The thick door kept her sniffling quiet, but Eli imagined it anyway.

"Please."

The door opened, but Meg didn't stand there. Eli pushed the door open a bit further and let it settle, searching for Meg in the dark room. He found her standing with her back to him, silhouetted in the window.

"I'm coming in."

"That's why I unlocked the door."

Eli entered the room and shut the door. The only light came from a small lamp on the bedside table, which cast her in golden hues, making her dark hair shine like oil. He wanted to take her into his arms and whisper words of comfort. Touch his lips to the hollow behind her ear and reassure her that he was there, that he'd shield her from anything unpleasant.

So many thoughts ran through his mind, and he wasn't sure now was the time for any of them to be vocalized. He moved forward and wrapped his arms around her, whispering, "I'm so sorry. Everything's going to be okay."

Even living half of his fantasy felt wonderful, and he pressed his cheek to hers, enjoying the shape of her body in front of his. "I really like you, Meg, and I don't want you to quit being Stockton's nanny."

She twisted in his arms, her eyes finding his and locking on. "You've always liked me."

"That I have." He smiled at her softly. "But this is a different kind of like," he said. "This is the kind that makes my heart beat weirdly and my mouth go dry and my mind make up ways I can get you alone so I can...." He swallowed, his gaze dropping to her mouth. "Kiss you," he finished hoarsely.

"Eli—"

"We could be a family," he said, his desperation rising no matter how he tried to tamp it down.

Meg's tears fell again as she shook her head. "I can't have kids, Eli. I can't be a mother. No mother." Her face scrunched up in pain. "No family."

Eli held her tight even when she tried to pull away. "Sh." She laid her head against his chest and cried, and Eli let her emotions rage out of her until she quieted.

"It wouldn't be a traditional family," he said, allowing her to step back, knowing she liked her space.

"Eli, we've spent countless hours together, right?"

"Right."

"So I've heard you say lots of times that you want more kids. I can't give you that."

Eli didn't know what to say or what to do. "Maybe I just need to re-evaluate what I want."

She nodded, resignation flashing across her face. "We probably both do." She hugged herself and looked away.

"What does that mean?"

"It's time for dinner." Meg wiped her eyes. "I need a few minutes to redo my makeup."

"You look beautiful."

She rolled her eyes and half-sobbed, half-scoffed. "Go on. I'll meet you in there."

Eli took a few steps away, then turned back. "You're coming, right?"

"Yeah, I think I've caused enough drama for one night."

"Not your fault," he said, considering her. His heart did that weird thing, and his mouth turned dry, and he closed the distance between them again, sweeping one arm around Meg's waist and pulling her close.

"See you out there." He pressed his lips to her temple, nowhere near her mouth like he'd imagined doing. "It's going to be a great Christmas, okay?"

Meg nodded, leaning into him for a few extra moments. "I just need—"

"A few minutes. I know. I'll wait for you in the hall."

"You don't need—"

"Meg. I haven't been in a relationship for a very long time." He swallowed, wondering what exactly he was saying. "But I know enough not to leave you to come into the dining room by yourself." He ducked his head and pushed his hat further onto his head. "See you in a minute."

He ducked back into the hall and pressed his back against the door, finally taking a deep, cleansing breath. Everything he'd said streamed through his mind, and he wasn't sure if he'd just done the right thing or made the biggest mistake of his life.

EIGHT

MEG SAT next to Stockton at dinner, and the name plate on the other side of her was Laney. The woman engaged Meg in a conversation about her life in Bora Bora, the children she'd looked after before getting hired by Eli, and what she was looking forward to in the new year.

Honestly, Meg's gratitude for the woman swelled, and her love for her did too. It took a special person to be able to cut right through the awkwardness as if it wasn't even there. She kept her attention on Stockton if he needed help or Laney, not even trying to extend her conversation to someone else or yell to be heard across the table.

A swell of noise went up, and she turned to see what the hubbub was about. Bree stood at the end of the table, under the archway that led into the hall—and directly under a sprig of mistletoe that hadn't been there when Meg had come to dinner.

"Kiss her," Graham called, and Meg realized that Eli sat directly next to Bree. Meg had come in with him, but the name plates must be honored, and she hadn't wanted to sit with him anyway. She needed some breathing room, some time to process everything he'd said, all she'd told him, and what she believed.

Eli waved his brother's demand away, his face turning bright red. "No, no."

"Come on," Andrew started. "No excuses, remember?"

"That wasn't even here when we sat down," Eli protested, his eyes landing on Meg's. She ducked her chin so he had to look somewhere else. She didn't need any more drama today. She also didn't need to watch him kiss another brunette right in front of her.

Bree stood there, laughing, her dark locks falling over her shoulder in gloriously perfect waves. Meg would kill for hair like that, but she didn't have it so she wore hers short.

"Come on," Beau called. "It's just a kiss."

It wouldn't be just a kiss to Meg—or to Eli. The man hadn't even been on one date since the death of his wife. As far as Meg knew he hadn't even had a crush on a woman since.

"Kiss her, kiss her," the brothers started chanting. Meg's mother lifted her roll to her mouth as if she were deaf and couldn't hear the Whittaker ruckus surrounding her. Amanda caught Meg's eye with sorrow in hers, and Meg wanted to bolt again.

So everyone knew about her feelings for Eli. *You haven't tried to hide them, at least recently*, she thought.

Finally Eli stood, his face set on angry, the flush there probably more from fury than anything else. He grabbed Bree with both hands and bent her back, much to his brothers' delight. They whooped and cheered as he kissed her, but all Meg could think was that she'd never be able to unsee that embrace.

Eli righted Bree and glared at everyone sitting at the table, Meg included. Then he stomped out of the dining room as the noise died down.

Meg pushed her peas around on her plate, wishing the ground would open up and swallow her whole. Laney's hand covered hers, and that unleashed a wave of emotion Meg wouldn't be able to hold back even if she tried her hardest.

So she didn't try. She looked at Laney, sure all the hurt, the jealousy, and the desperation were plain for the other woman to see.

"Don't worry about it," Laney whispered, reaching up to wipe Meg's eyes. "He likes you, Meg. He'll come around."

Meg never was one to kiss and tell, so she didn't say anything about Eli's confessions to her. She still wasn't sure what she believed and if his timing was genuine.

Coffee and cider got served, and Celia made Stockton move down a chair so she could have the one right next to Meg. She put one arm around her shoulder, and Meg wanted to lean into her and have a good cry.

"Come on, dear." Celia stood and left the dining room, hardly anyone watching her. But when Meg got up, it seemed like every eye zoomed to her. The chatter died as if Meg herself had killed it.

She managed to keep her tears dormant until she joined Celia in her big bedroom upstairs. Then she curled into the older woman—the woman who had become so much like the mother Meg had always wanted—and cried.

SHE WOKE in the middle of the night, disoriented and afraid. *This isn't my bedroom*, she thought, sitting up wildly and trying to get her bearings. Another body slumbered beside her, and she still wore her clothes from earlier.

She'd fallen asleep in Celia's bed, and the other woman had clearly let her stay.

Meg didn't want to leave, didn't want to go creeping down the stairs in the middle of the night so she could sleep in a room only a wall away from the man who she simultaneously wanted to spend a lot of time with and never wanted to see again.

Confused, she lay back down and stared toward the gray rectangle that indicated the window. Her face felt dry, crackly, and puffy, and she wiped her hand down her cheek, wishing she felt normal. Wondering what that even felt like, and if she'd be able to get back to that place again.

She dozed until Celia stirred, which also woke her. Meg moved to the edge of the bed and paused, feeling more tired now than she had last night, unsure if that was even possible.

"I thought you were spending Christmas with your family," Meg said.

"I am," Celia said. "I'm just sliding a couple of casseroles in the oven and I'm heading out."

Their eyes met, and Meg said, "You're too good to this family."

Celia gave her a small smile and came over to press her lips to Meg's forehead. "They're a good family. I'll see you in a couple of days, but you call me if you need anything." She gripped Meg's shoulders and gave her a slight shake. "Okay?"

Meg nodded though she knew she wouldn't be calling Celia unless there was a major catastrophe. Of course, with her mother here, a catastrophe might just happen. Meg showered in Celia's attached bathroom and went downstairs with damp hair and no makeup to find the kitchen already hopping with people, conversation, and food.

She didn't feel like being a zoo animal again, so she bypassed the festivities and headed down the hall toward her room. Before she even reached the office where Graham and Eli worked, Stockton called, "Meggy," and she turned around.

"Hey, bud. Did you guys open presents yet?"

"No, Daddy wouldn't let us until you came down."

Meg looked up to find Eli standing at the far entrance to the kitchen, his arms folded across his chest. He wore a pair of black sweats that somehow looked like a tuxedo on him and a light blue T-shirt that strained across his chest and through his biceps. Even from several feet away, he looked exhausted.

"You didn't have to wait for me," she said.

"Sure we did." Eli flashed a smile that barely stayed on his face long enough to see. "Let me get the others." He walked back into the kitchen and everyone came spilling out into the foyer, where the Christmas tree shined it's colored lights down on dozens and dozens of presents.

Meg really didn't feel all that jolly, but she didn't see how she could skip out on the present opening, especially as it seemed Eli had made his entire family wait for her. She tucked herself into a corner of the room while Amanda took the lead in handing out all the gifts. The Whittakers then went around in a circle, opening one present at a time and showing it to the group.

Meg had five presents—one from Eli, one from Stockton, one from Amanda, one from Celia, and one from

Laney and Graham. She loved her new fuzzy socks with grips on the soles from Stockton, and the gift card for ebooks Amanda had bought for her. Laney and Graham had provided a gift certificate to the salon, and Celia had bought a baking cookbook that Meg leafed through while she waited for her turn to come around again.

Only Eli's present remained, and she hoped he wouldn't be stupid enough to give her something intimate she'd have to open in front of his whole family. At the same time, if it was something too impersonal, she felt sure her raisin of a heart would harden into a stone.

Her heart started skipping around like a frog when Stockton started unwrapping his next present. Eli had given him a painting set, and the boy laughed and launched himself into his dad's arms.

Laney went again, and she opened an envelope from Eli that Meg knew was about the horse. Sure enough, Laney sucked in a breath and said, "Eli, you did not."

"What?" Graham took the papers Laney handed to him, and Meg saw the colorful crayon Stockton had obviously used to make their card. "A horse?"

Laney jumped up, her face the picture of happiness as she embraced Eli. "Can we go meet her now?"

"I don't think we're done with the presents."

But Meg jumped to her feet too. "I'll get our winter clothes out. Come on, Stocky." She extended her hand toward the little boy and he put his sweet fingers in hers.

"Do I have to wear the scarf, Meggy? It itches."

"Depends on how hard the wind's blowing, bud. It keeps your neck from freezing." The party broke up, but Meg caught the look of displeasure on Eli's face as he silently watched everyone file past him.

"Meg," he tried, but she shook her head and nudged Stockton toward the mud room to get suited up to go out into the winter cold. The barns and stables at Whiskey Mountain Lodge sat down a path that Eli kept shoveled, past the yard, the volleyball courts, the swimming pool, and the strawberry patch.

It was a couple of blocks at most, and Meg usually liked making the walk, rain or shine. Snow or sun. She felt close to God out under the sky here in Wyoming, the peace in the quiet atmosphere, the scent of the oxygen here clean and crisp.

Today, though, with everyone tromping down there in a single-file line, it felt like a chore to walk that far. But she stayed behind Stockton so she didn't have to go too fast, and so she didn't have to walk by Eli.

She'd grown up around cowboys and horses, and the scent of hay and feed made her think of her childhood. Eli led Laney and Graham over to a beautiful red sorrel horse and said, "Ta-da."

"I named 'im Blue Moon," Stockton said.

Graham scooped the little boy up. "He's red, buddy."

Stockton looked confused and he looked from Graham to the horse. "My dad said we could name him whatever."

"I was under some stress," Eli muttered.

"It's a fine name," Laney said, running her hand along the horse's nose and face to scratch the animal behind its ears. She beamed at the animal, and Meg wondered if she loved anything as much as Laney loved horses.

Kids, probably.

Graham set Stockton down and joined his wife at the stable door, with Andrew and Beau crowding around as if they'd never seen a horse before.

"I have to go to the bathroom," Stockton said, tugging on her hand, and Meg turned with him to leave.

But Amanda said, "I'll take him," and slipped her hand into the little boy's. "Come on, bud. Grandma's too cold out here."

"I'm not even wearing my scarf," Stockton said like he was tough for leaving the itchy article of clothing behind. Meg watched them walk away, starting to feel the chill herself. She startled when a warm hand touched her cold one, and she started to pull away from the electric charge. Eli held her fast and wouldn't let her retreat from him.

"Let's take a walk," he said, gently tugging her away from the stables but not back toward the lodge.

"I'm cold, Eli."

"We won't go far," he promised. She expected him to say something about last night's kiss, about something he'd said last night, something. But he just walked, their hands swinging easily between them.

"You didn't open my gift," he finally said.

"Laney opened the horse first." Meg shrugged with one shoulder and kept her eyes on the frosted trees up ahead. "What was it?"

Eli chuckled. "Yeah, I'm not telling you, and as soon as we get back to the lodge, you're opening it."

She sighed and paused. "It's not...romantic, is it?"

Eli gazed at her with adoration in his eyes, and Meg didn't know what to do with it.

"I didn't want to kiss Bree," he said. "It was just good fun."

"Sure," Meg said. "But I don't think you believe that."

"Why not?"

"Because, Eli, I've worked for you for four years, and you have never once gone out with a woman. Or even looked at a woman." She took a deep breath. "So I know that kiss made you angry, and it made me angry too."

"I'm looking at you," he said, swallowing. "And I want to kiss you."

Meg's frustration evaporated instantly and her heart thumped wildly against her ribs, cheering at the very thought of kissing Eli.

"There's no mistletoe," she whispered as he dipped his head closer to hers.

"None needed," he murmured just before grazing her cheek with his lips. If he called that a kiss, Meg was going to have to educate him on how to kiss a girl. "Is this okay?" he asked.

"Honestly, Eli, I feel like a yo-yo." She exhaled out a small laugh. "Up one minute and down the next. Wanting you one moment and not wanting you the next." She leaned into his embrace, every nerve heightened in anticipation.

"Where are we right now?"

"I'd say up."

"So kissing is okay?"

Meg had dreamed about kissing him so often, she was actually worried the real thing would be worse than her imagination. "Eli, if you don't kiss me in the next ten seconds, I'm going back to the lodge alone."

He swept his cowboy hat off in one quick movement and held her tighter. He paused for another moment, and Meg saw indecision and pain and hope and love in his eyes all at the same time. "I haven't kissed someone in a long time," he said, swallowing again.

"Sure you have. Last night." A smile touched her lips as she reached up and ran her fingers through his hair. He closed his eyes and lowered his head, not nearly far enough to kiss her.

So Meg stretched up and closed the distance between them, finally matching her mouth to his. Fireworks exploded from the heat of his touch, from the gentle press of his lips to hers, and the way he slowly explored before deepening the kiss.

And while he hadn't kissed a woman for real in a long time, he sure knew how to do it.

He pulled back, putting a hair of space between them. "Okay?"

Oh, that kiss was better than okay. Better than her fantasies too. Meg felt warm from head to toe, and all she wanted was to kiss him again. So she did.

NINE

NINETY PERCENT of Eli really enjoyed kissing Meg, something he'd been thinking about doing for weeks. Ten percent of him wondered if he was doing the right thing, if he was cheating on Caroline, if he should be having a relationship with his nanny.

But that ten percent was easy to silence with the scent of Meg in his nose, the shape of her body beside his, and the way she loved his son.

Wrong reasons, he thought as he continued to kiss her. He felt positively steamy in the cold, Christmas morning, and when Meg broke their second kiss and giggled, Eli swayed on his feet.

You like her too, he thought as he opened his eyes to the brightness of the snow. And he did. He liked her a whole lot.

"Stockton wants to go snowshoeing later. You want to come?"

"Of course." Meg turned toward the lodge and dropped her hand to his again. "But I need to eat first."

"Oh, that's right. Sleeping Beauty didn't eat breakfast yet." He chuckled and bumped her with his hip.

"Oh my goodness. My mother." She wore a panicked expression Eli wanted to soothe. "Where's my mother?"

"She was still sleeping too," Eli said. "Guess it runs in the family."

Meg increased her pace, and Eli went with her, the distinct thought that she'd been following him around all these years but that he was pretty sure he'd go wherever she wanted him to at this point.

He really wanted her to open his Christmas gift so he could see her face. And he hadn't opened her present yet either, and he was dying to know what was in the slim box he knew had come from her because of the big black M scrawled on the paper.

He hadn't exactly saved it for last, but they really hadn't finished opening their presents before they'd all taken a trip out to the stables.

In the lodge, he stripped off his coat and kicked off his boots. Meg had bundled up with a hat, scarf, boots, and a coat, so she took a little longer than him. He waited just outside the mudroom, not wanting her to escape to check on her mom before they finished the gifts.

He glanced into the kitchen, where his mom had just

finished scooping a serving of French toast casserole for Stockton. "Your mom's in here," he said, nodding toward the kitchen.

Meg joined him at the corner of the wall, and he should've stepped back. But he wanted her in his personal space, and she tensed as she checked on her mother, who sat at the bar beside Stockton with only eggs on her plate.

His mom turned and smiled at them. "There's plenty left to eat," she said.

"We're going to finish the presents first." Eli smiled and laced his fingers through Meg's.

His mother catalogued the motion and her eyes flicked up. "Oh, watch out, hon. You're standing in a delicate place." She pointed up, and Eli followed her finger to see that blasted mistletoe taped crudely to the arch leading into the mudroom.

Heat filled him, and he was eternally glad he'd kissed her somewhere else for the first time. He wouldn't want that first kiss to be a show. Not that his mother would make him kiss Meg just because they stood under a weed.

"Come on." Eli tugged Meg past the kitchen and into the foyer on the other side of the wall. "You open mine first." He picked up the box, his anticipation practically eating him from the inside out.

She took the box and shook it, but it didn't make a sound, and she narrowed her eyes. "This feels like it doesn't have anything in it."

"Well, it does." Eli's nerves felt like he'd put them

through a woodchipper, not that he'd actually used one of those before.

Meg gave him a sexy, coy look as she ripped off the paper. She focused on her task as she opened the box and pulled out the few pages he'd stapled together. Her eyes held anxiety as she read, as she made sense of what she was seeing.

Her eyes came to his, wide and surprised. "These are tickets to Disneyland."

"That's right." Eli grinned at her. "You must've told me a hundred times that you've never been." He tucked his hands into his pockets. "So now you can go."

She examined the pages again. "There are three tickets here."

Eli swallowed, his throat so, so dry. He was probably being too presumptuous. Too forward. Too...something. "Uh, yeah." He rocked back on his heels. "I thought the three of us could go. Sort of a vacation when we get sick of the snow." He shrugged like it was no big deal to him, but honestly, it was. He'd been to Disneyland—had season tickets when he and Caroline lived in California.

He took a couple of steps toward Meg and said, "I haven't been back to California since...." He swallowed again, wondering if he was developing some sort of medical condition. "Since Caroline died."

Meg looked at him again. "Oh, Eli." She reached out and cradled his face. "Thank you. I'm so excited to go, and Stockton will love it." She beamed at him with adoration he wasn't sure he deserved. She blinked and said, "Okay, open mine."

He noticed she kept a tight grip on the tickets as she bent to pick up the box he'd left behind.

"It's dumb," she said. "You buy whatever you want. But—" She shrugged. "It's the thought that counts, right?" She practically thrust the box at him, and Eli took it from her, glad his gift had been well-received.

He shook her gift too, laughing when she rolled her eyes. It looked like a tie box he'd get from an expensive men's wear store. And that's what it was. He met her eye, wondering if she'd really bought him a tie. He hoped not. It felt...impersonal.

He opened the tie box and pulled out a tie, but not the kind he wore around his neck. This one had been hand-crafted out of gift cards.

"So that's to The Devil's Tower," she said, pointing as if he'd suddenly turned illiterate and couldn't read. "I know you like their food. And one to that drink place you drive through every time you go to town. And one for that cookie place that'll deliver."

Some of the cards had been trimmed so they all fit into the shape of a tie, and Eli held it up to his throat, laughing. "It's perfect, Meg. Thank you." He swept his arm around her waist and brought her close, sobering as the moment turned charged.

He brushed his lips against hers, seeking permission though he'd kissed her already. She gave it by leaning into him and making the kiss more substantial. "Merry Christmas," he whispered just before the back door opened and a whole ruckus of sound came inside.

Meg stepped out of his embrace, her head down but not so far that Eli couldn't see her smile. So maybe he wasn't as rusty as he'd thought, though he still felt light years out of his element when it came to dating and women.

"What're you two doing in here?" Andrew asked, taking in the whole scene before him as if he could see back in time and know what happened here.

"Just finishing with the presents," Eli said. "And now we're going to go eat." He guided Meg past his squinty-eyed brother, but Andrew put his hand on Eli's chest, stopping him before he could pass.

"Seriously?"

Eli shrugged. "Among other things." He grinned and patted Andrew on the shoulder as he followed Meg into the kitchen.

ELI WORKED in the barn while his son followed behind him with a broom that Eli had cut the handle down on so it was child-sized. "Be sure to get into the corners, bud."

Stockton kept humming, the swish-swish of his broom almost like a beat box to go with his voice. Eli brushed down the last horse and checked the tack room. Every horse had been fed and watered and cared for, and still Meg hadn't come out of the lodge.

At this point, he seriously wondered if she would, and Eli didn't have a whole lot left to give Stockton to do. He'd told Stockton they could go snowshoeing as soon as the stables were clean, and Eli glanced around, wondering if he should just go with his son.

"Come on, bud," he said. "Let's get the shoes, and you're going to have to put on your scarf."

The fact that Stockton didn't complain about the scratchy scarf and practically ran to the corner to put his broom away testified of his eagerness to go. He took his snowshoes from Eli and sat down on the bench to strap the shoes to his boots. They'd moved to Wyoming in the dead of winter last year, and snowshoeing had fast become one of Stockton's favorite things.

Eli had bought the boy his own shoes, and sometimes he wore them around the yard as he made snowmen.

"Ready, Dad." Stockton stood, his stance just a bit wider than normal because of the wider frames of the snowshoes.

"Yeah." Eli glanced toward the door at the other end of the stable, but Meg didn't come through it. He pulled out his phone and called her, saying to Stockton, "Let me see if Meg is coming with us."

"She doesn't like snowshoeing," Stockton said matter-of-factly.

Eli blinked at his son as the line rang. "She doesn't?"

"She said she likes cross-country skiing better." Stockton looked up at him. "I like the snowshoes." He smiled and wrapped the scarf around his neck, his indication that he was ready to go.

Meg finally said, "Hello?" in a breathless voice. "Eli?"

"Hey, so, Stockton and I are just heading out on the snowshoes. Were...you coming?"

"Oh! The snowshoeing. Yes. Yes, I am coming to that."

Eli smiled and motioned for Stockton to go outside and wait for him. "Okay, well, we're down at the stables."

"I'm on my way. I just need to tell my mom."

Eli turned toward the door and held it open for Stockton as he clomped out. "How's your mom?"

"She's doing okay, actually. Andrew and Beau got her playing cards, and now she's teaching them how to play cribbage." She laughed, and Eli was glad to hear some joy in her voice. "I'm putting my boots on now."

Sure enough, she came through the door eight minutes later, fully equipped for shoeing through the snow. Eli's whole face broke into a huge smile and he kept himself from lunging toward her. He walked normally and drew her into a hug. "Good to see you."

"You too." She tucked her hair into her hat, her cheeks already pink from the cold.

He got her a pair of shoes and helped her strap them on, then he did the same. They joined Stockton, who had been walking around on the snow outside the stables.

"You ready, Stocky?" Meg called, and Stockton perked right up.

"Yeah, can we do the pine trail?"

Meg looked at Eli, and he said, "It's not bad. Through the trees. Maybe a half an hour out and then half an hour back."

She nodded, and Eli said, "Yeah, bud, lead us toward the trail."

Meg wasn't particularly skilled at snowshoeing, but he let her go after Stockton and Eli brought up the rear. With the bulky winter gear and Meg's general clumsiness in the shoes, Eli opted to keep the conversation at a minimum.

He simply enjoyed being out in God's country, the huge Teton mountains towering over them, the tops concealed among the clouds that had rolled in while he and Stockton had cleaned the stables.

They finally reached the century-old pines the trail was named after, and Eli noticed that Meg was red-faced, sweating, and breathless. A twinge of guilt hit him. If it was true she didn't like snowshoeing....

"Can I take my shoes off, Dad?"

"Where you gonna go?" Eli asked.

"Just around the trees. Uncle Graham showed me some owl nests last time we came out here." Stockton bent and started undoing the clasp keeping his boot on the snowshoe. "There's hardly any snow because of the trees."

"I guess so." Eli said, because Stockton already had one boot free. He doubted anything he said would deter the boy, and it was just snowshoes, so what did it matter? Stockton grinned and ran off, pulling something from his pocket as he did.

"What does he have?" Meg asked, standing straight and still and tall.

"I have no idea." Eli sighed. "And he's only six. Can you imagine what he'll be like when he's sixteen?" He shook his head and chuckled, glad when Meg joined in.

"Oh, he'll be fine." Meg stutter-stepped over to Eli and laced her arm through his. "He's got a great dad." She gazed up at him with those deep, dark eyes, and Eli felt himself slipping, sliding, tripping, tumbling down the slope toward falling in love with her.

"I think you spend more time with him than I do," Eli murmured.

"Mm." Meg's eyes drifted closed and she leaned further into him, her wishes crystal clear. Eli kissed her, finding her mouth soft and supple, the scent of her combining with the taste of her lips and almost igniting his blood.

Her fingernails traced along the back of his neck, making him shiver. He pulled her as close as he could with the bulky, awkward snowshoes, wishing he'd taken his off like his son had.

When he finally pulled away, he felt more complete than he had since Caroline's death.

"So, cowboy." Meg kept herself right beside Eli, her

face only inches from his. "When do you think we should tell Stockton about us?"

"You think we need to have a specific conversation about it?"

She stopped leaning into him and met his eyes with a hint of alarm in hers. "Yes. Don't you?"

"He's six."

"And he's smart. He knows I'm not his mother." She pressed her lips together. "And I'll never be a mother."

Curiosity tugged at Eli. "What happened, Meg?" He hoped they were to a place in their relationship where they could have real, meaningful conversations.

"I had some complications from a surgery when I was a teenager," she said. "I was losing a lot of blood, and my mother decided to have the doctor perform a complete hysterectomy." She drifted away from him, both physically and emotionally, and Eli watched her go.

"I was fifteen," she said. "I think that's why I've always felt this call to be a nanny."

"Is that...? I mean, you don't get along with your mother." He shrugged, but Meg wasn't even looking at him.

"I probably wouldn't have been able to get pregnant anyway." Her voice carried a ghost from the past, filled with some strange note Eli didn't like and wanted to erase. "My endometriosis was complete, and painful, and...yeah."

Eli stepped toward her and wrapped his arms around her, unwilling to let her sift through her memories without something to hold on to. He knew what that was like, and he never liked thinking about Caroline when he was alone. It was too easy to fall down a rabbit hole of self-loathing, regret, and anger.

"You've been a good mother to Stockton," he whispered in her ear. "And we can talk to him whenever. Maybe after your mom goes home?"

Meg nodded and Eli held her, the sweet silence in the snow almost perfect. If only there wasn't still that nagging thought that he was doing something wrong. But being with Meg felt right. He'd never have his whole heart to give her, as Caroline had claimed some of it and taken it with her when she'd died.

But he could still love, he knew that.

He pushed the uncomfortable feelings away. Whatever it was, he'd figure it out and overcome it, because he sure liked being with Meg and having the promise of a family with her and Stockton.

TEN

MEG MADE her decision as soon as Stockton came skipping around the pine trees. She wouldn't be quitting. She couldn't let go of that little boy, with his flop of brown hair and the bright blue eyes he'd inherited from his mother.

She loved him, and she thought she might be falling for Eli too—her crush seemed to have developed more than legs over the past few days. A seed of fear seemed stuck in the back of her mind, and she couldn't let go of it. It sprouted and grew, and she'd hack it back, and it would wither for a while, only to return with a vengeance.

It hadn't died yet, and she wasn't sure what it would take to get it to leave completely. The way Eli had just kissed her should've done it. He was so tender, so soft, and yet so insistent at the same time. She'd never felt as cherished as she did while standing in Eli's embrace, and she prayed for a happy ending to this situation.

And get me back to the lodge safely, she added, realizing she had another half an hour of snowshoeing before she could truly relax. She didn't understand that allure of the activity, but Stockton loved it, and Meg wanted to spend time with Eli. So she'd come, though she'd have preferred they put on a movie in the theater room downstairs and pop a bunch of popcorn in the mini kitchen in the basement.

"Ready?" Eli asked his son, snapping Meg out of her inner thoughts. Her muscles tensed as Stockton straightened and gave them both a thumbs-up.

She wondered how Stockton would take the news of her and his dad dating. She'd learned it was always best to be up-front with children about things, even sensitive subjects. They didn't need to know everything, or be exposed to adult situations, but they did have opinions, and they should be listened to.

Back at the lodge, Laney and Graham had returned from their family lunch, and Bailey came skipping out to meet Stockton. "My mom wants to know if everyone wants to watch a movie."

Meg didn't miss a beat when she said, "I do."

"We're in," Eli also said, but Stockton groaned.

"Maybe if it's not one of those dumb ones," he said as he kicked the snow off his boots against the hose.

"What makes a dumb one?" Meg asked.

"I don't know." He went through the door Eli held

open and dumped his coat and boots and gloves and everything on the mudroom floor.

"Hey, hang that up," Eli said when he entered, but Stockton had already run off with Bailey. Meg bent over and collected the child's gear and started putting it all on hooks and shelves where it belonged.

"You don't have to do that." Eli made a swipe for Stockton's coat, snatching it right out of Meg's hand.

She froze. "All right. I don't mind." In fact, he'd paid her a lot of money over the past four years to do exactly what she'd been doing. She helped Stockton with his homework while Eli sat at the same table, looking at something on his phone. She got Stockton ready for school, taught him how to tie his shoes, made sure he had a lunch if he needed one, all while Eli got himself ready just in time to kiss the top of Stockton's head before Meg drove him to school.

Sometimes Laney drove, and Meg would stand in the doorway until the little boy was loaded up and off. No matter what, when she turned back to the lodge, it was to do laundry, make Stockton's bed, and make sure the Whittaker's had food in the house.

Sure, Graham still employed Annie to clean, and Bree to decorate, and Celia to cook. But Meg was just as much an employee of the Whittaker family as they were.

Frustration dove through her as she removed her coat and gloves and hung everything up. The kitchen table where Beau and Andrew had been playing cribbage with her mom had been abandoned, the game still set up.

She cocked her head at the cards and slim board with the pegs still poking out of it. "Where do you think they went?"

"Basement?" Eli guessed as he came around the corner from the mudroom. "I'm going to go check on a few things before I come down." His hand slipped along her waist, touching her but not staying long. He moved down the hall and into the office, and Meg didn't want to go downstairs by herself.

But Stockton was down there...and her mother, most likely. So she went in the opposite direction and down the steps behind the giant Christmas tree in the foyer. A yawn widened her mouth and she paused on the steps until she had her footing. A bit dizzy, she continued downstairs and found the party had indeed moved down here.

The counter in the kitchen was covered with chips and cookies and cans of soda. The theater room boasted a sound-proof door, but it wasn't closed. The music from the movie inside nearly knocked Meg off her feet, but she continued on to make sure her responsibilities were covered before she went to take a nap.

Sure enough, Stockton sat in a huge recliner with Bailey, and Meg told him that his dad was upstairs if he needed anything.

"I'll keep an eye on him," Laney said from where she was cuddled into Graham's side. "And your mom."

Meg smiled and said, "Thanks, Laney," before turning to her mom. "You'll be okay down here?"

"Fine, fine."

"I didn't sleep well last night, so I'm going ot go lie down in my bedroom." Meg leaned over and placed a kiss on her mother's cheek, a bit surprised at the action. Her mom was obviously surprised too, because she looked at Meg then—really looked at her.

"Why didn't you sleep well?"

Meg didn't want to get into everything from how her mother had spilled her infertility to the entire family to how she'd had to watch Eli kiss another woman. Not only that, she'd taken comfort from Celia, not her mother, and that was another issue Meg needed to deal with. Or maybe she didn't. She wasn't exactly sure. She just knew she was tired and didn't want to watch whatever action flick they had amping up on the big screen.

"Pull that door closed, would you, Meg?" Andrew asked as she passed him, and she did, sealing the light out and the sound in. She snagged a cookie on her way past the counter and went back upstairs.

She poked her head into Eli's office and said, "They're all in the basement watching some movie with great big robots. Lots of fun snacks down there, though." She lifted the last bite of her cookie before popping it into her mouth.

Eli glanced up from his laptop. "Do you have a sec?"

"Sure, I was just going to take a nap." She stepped into

the office instead, surprised and a bit worried when Eli got up and closed the door before facing her. "What's going on?"

"I need to know if you were serious about quitting," he said.

She hated it when he adopted his business persona with her. So she cocked her hip and put one hand on it to give him some sass back. "No, Eli. I've decided I can't leave Stockton."

His whole face lit up with hope. "Are you serious?"

Meg sighed and looked away, toward Graham's messy desk. "Yeah, I'm serious."

Eli whooped and she barely had time to look at him again before he caught her around the waist. "He'll be so happy. Heck, *I'm* happy." He set her on her feet again and kissed her, this time with less tenderness and a little more oomph behind the movement.

Meg liked nothing more than kissing Eli, and she lost herself to the taste and touch of him, slightly drunk when he pulled away. "Thank you so much, Meggy." He bounced back over to his desk and shut his laptop. "I'll be downstairs. You sure you don't want to come snuggle with me?"

Still reeling from his gratitude, Meg managed to shake her head. "Too obvious."

Eli laughed. "As if everyone doesn't already know."

The thought only made Meg cringe away from putting

herself in Eli's arms where everyone could see. "Not Stockton."

A cloud passed over Eli's face, and then he nodded. "All right. Enjoy your nap." He took a step as if he'd go around her, but she blocked him.

"You didn't—I mean, are you only—did you only kiss me so I'd stay here and be Stockton's nanny?"

Eli looked like she'd thrown ice water in his face. "What? No."

But Meg cocked her head, trying to hear between the letters he'd spoken. "It feels weird, doesn't it? You paying me to take care of him, but kissing me in secret? Like, I don't want to be that kind of girl."

"You're not that kind of girl." Emotions warred their way across Eli's face, and Meg could see that not everything was as black and white as they'd like it to be.

"You're going to keep paying me, right?"

"Yes."

Meg relaxed a little, but the situation hadn't changed. "Is this weird? Or am I just...I don't know."

"I don't know either." Eli's earlier happiness had fled, and Meg hated that she'd done that.

"Maybe I should quit. Then you can pay someone you aren't kissing."

"You can't quit." He exhaled harshly. "People meet and date at work all the time."

"Not the boss and his employee." This back and forth was the exact reason Meg had always kept her crush in the simple stages—and secret. Kissing and holding hands, they complicated everything.

"Yes, the boss and his employee," Eli said. "You're doing your job. We just happen to have a relationship on the side."

"So maybe we shouldn't kiss while I'm working."

"Sure, if that's what you want. It's Christmas Day." He stepped toward her, an edge of desire driving away the frustration that had entered his gaze. "You're not on the clock today. That's why I didn't want you picking up his coat and stuff."

Meg giggled as he drew her into his arms. "You keep telling yourself that, Mister Whittaker."

"What? It's true." He gazed into her eyes. "And I'm going to kiss you again, because tomorrow you'll be back at work, and I won't get to do it." He did, and this kiss held something just a bit different for Meg. What it was, she couldn't say, but there was definitely something new there. When Eli pulled back, he didn't smile at her, didn't have that soft look of adoration or love in his eyes.

It was almost like he was analyzing a high-profile proposal he'd written for a big event at one of the resorts where he'd worked. She'd often go over them with him, to help him win the events and bring more business to the hotels.

"Okay," he said, accompanied with a nervous chuckle. "I'm gonna head downstairs, and...." He moved to step past her and they ended up going the same direction, performing a sort of strange little dance filled with awkwardness.

Meg finally put her hands on his shoulders, trying not to feel the muscles beneath his shirt. "You go this way." She sort of pushed him to the right while she went left. "And I'll go this way."

Eli laughed, breaking the tension in the room. He grabbed onto Meg and twirled her around, causing her to laugh too. He paused, and now when he looked down at her, it was with all those emotions she'd come to expect from him.

"I really like you," he murmured, and those words were almost as good as his tender, insistent kisses.

LATER THAT NIGHT, with snow falling outside the windows of the lodge, Meg took her mug of hot chocolate to the table, where another rousing game of cribbage had just started. Beau and Andrew had teamed up against Meg's mother, but they still hadn't managed to beat her yet.

"It's just the luck of the cards," she'd said on the last one, her face a mask of pure joy. Meg had literally never seen her mom look so happy. She'd existed in misery for so long, Meg thought she must like feeling that way.

When they lost again, and Andrew threw up his hands

with, "I don't know how she does it!" her mom turned to her.

"Want to try, Meg?"

Andrew and Beau turned toward her, insane looks of hope in their eyes. "Can you beat her?" Beau asked.

"I don't think it's possible," Andrew said. "She's like a machine."

"It's just luck," her mom said, beaming. "Honest. Meg's beat me before."

"I haven't played cribbage in a long time," Meg said, holding up her hands. "I'm a master at Go Fish though. Or checkers. I'll play that."

"Meg," Andrew said, clapping his hands and exchanging a look with Beau. They must've had some sort of secret Whittaker brother language, because all of them —Beau, Andrew, and Eli all picked up the chant with the second, "Meg."

"Meg, Meg, Meg."

She rolled her eyes though pure giddiness romped through her. "I can't beat her," she said, but her voice was nowhere near loud enough to be heard over three men.

When Beau started pounding on the table in time with the chants, Meg picked up the deck of cards and shuffled them amidst cheering. Once it died down, she said, "I'm not going to win."

She dealt the cards to her mom and then herself while her mom moved all the pegs back to the starting line.

Laney brought another bowl of popcorn to the table and eased into a chair down on the end.

Meg met her eye, and Laney smiled as if to say, *See? What a difference twenty-four hours makes, right?*

After that, Meg concentrated, trying to make sure she laid away the right cards and playing things just right to add up in her favor. In the end, she shouldn't have dealt, because her mother got to count out first—and she won before Meg could even count.

"And that's two more." Her mom looked so happy as she moved her peg, and the rest of the crowd groaned. Everyone had gathered around to watch the epic match, and Stockton, who had climbed into Meg's lap about halfway through turned to her and gave her a big hug.

"Don't worry about it, Meggy. I can't beat Bailey at the racecar game."

"The racecar game?" She lifted her eyebrows at him and then looked at Laney.

"Oh, it's this video game we have," she said. "Bailey's been playing it for years and knows all the shortcuts."

Meg snuggled with Stockton and said, "It's okay when you lose to your mom. Or your best friend."

"Yeah, I guess so." Stockton turned back to the game, but no one else had picked up the cards.

Meg leaned into the little boy and said, "You should make her a crown before she goes." She caught her mother's eye, and something meaningful passed between them. Meg wondered if her mom had this kind of fun, happy, easy relationship with Carrie and Brittany. That was probably why they could stand having their mother over for all the holidays when Meg couldn't.

A moment of sadness pinched behind her lungs that she'd basically given up on her mother all those years ago. "I'm sorry," she said way too quietly for her mom to hear. But somehow the message was conveyed, and suddenly Meg wished her mom could stay for longer than one more day.

ELEVEN

THE OLD-SCHOOL LANDLINE phone rang on the desk where Eli worked. He looked at it for a moment, not quite sure when it had sounded last. Then he sprang into action and answered it, because it was the number he'd published for reservations at the boarding stable.

"The Whittaker...uh...Whiskey Mountain Stables." He pressed his eyes closed as a slip of foolishness stole through him. Most of their clients at the stables came through bookings at the lodge, so he was a bit out of practice.

Graham chuckled at the other desk, but Eli purposely turned away from him.

"I'd like to book eleven horses," a woman said. "For a day ride. My family and I are staying at the Grand Teton Lodge, but they don't have horses."

"Well, ma'am, we do, and if you'll tell me what dates

you and your family need the horses, I'll see what I've got." He only had two bookings on the ledger right now, and they were both for guests already staying at the lodge.

He pulled the pricing schedule toward him as she recited the dates, and he shoved his laptop off the desk calendar that contained the bookings for the stables and the lodge. That way, he didn't have to be present at the desk to take reservations.

"Let's see...." He clicked his tongue. "June sixteenth is available. Our fee for eleven horses for the day is six hundred dollars." He waited for the woman to haggle over the price, but she didn't. She simply agreed and gave him her credit card number so he could reserve the date and the horses with a non-refundable deposit.

He hung up, feeling very accomplished. While he didn't need to work for money, it was nice to actually achieve something.

"Oh, you're so proud of yourself." The teasing quality in Graham's voice eased the sting of the words a little bit.

"Well, we can't all run huge energy companies." Eli flicked his brother a glance but didn't give him his full attention. It had driven Graham—and their parents—crazy as a teenager. But Eli didn't have a whole lot to celebrate lately. Last winter, he hadn't really tried to do much more than buy more horses and make sure they were trained. He made sure Stockton was settling in okay and built a website for the stables, got brochures and pamphlets and other marketing materials ready.

If there was anything Eli was good at, it was marketing materials and advertising events. By the time spring came, he'd booked the stables for the entire summer. He'd visited other stables, interviewed their managers about the horses, their prices, all of it.

He'd been planning a big marketing push for after the new year, and this phone call proved that people planned their family reunions and camping trips months and months in advance.

"Andrew helps with Springside," Graham finally said, as if he'd been thinking of a comeback all this time.

"With the public relations." Eli refrained from rolling his eyes. His tone had suggested it already.

"And Dwight," Graham said. "I hardly do anything."

"Well, you sit at that desk a lot for not doing anything."

"So do you." Graham got up and came around the front of his desk before perching on the edge of it. "What's eating you?"

Meg. "Nothing." Eli positioned his laptop back in front of him, wishing he could iron his feelings flat so he could examine them more easily.

"You and Meg seemed to have a good Christmas."

"We did."

"Did you kiss her?"

Eli gave up his pretense of working and leaned back in his chair. "Yes, okay?"

Graham didn't grin or act like that was great news. He

folded his arms and said, "That's a big deal for you. What with Caroline and all."

Caroline. A knife twisted in Eli's gut, then his heart.

"Don't look like that," Graham said. "This is good, Eli. She really likes you, and you obviously like her."

"Yeah, I know." He wasn't sure Graham could understand his predicament. He'd spoken about it with his mom, who hadn't tried dating yet after the death of her husband. But she'd expressed some similar concerns to Eli, but hastened to say, "But you're so young, honey. And Stockton would thrive with a mother."

He'd wanted to tell her that Meg was the best surrogate mother he could provide for his son. But was she the best match for him?

"It's not like you'll get remarried tomorrow," Graham said. "Enjoy yourself. Go slow. Kiss her a lot." That smile Eli had expected sprang to Graham's face. "Don't *worry* so much."

"Easy for you to say." Eli stood and stretched his back. "And I know I'm not getting remarried tomorrow. We're driving Meg's mom back to Colorado tomorrow." He gave Graham a smirk and said, "I'm going out to the stables."

Graham chuckled. "Gonna go tell your secrets to Second to Caroline?"

Eli yanked open the office door. "That's right." He didn't wait for Graham to continue ribbing him, or giving him advice, even if it was useful. Eli had been the first brother to find a wife, and it felt wildly unfair that Caroline had been taken from him.

As he pulled on his boots and zipped his coat, he wondered when he was going to stop thinking life was unfair.

Help me be grateful for what I have, he thought as he exited the lodge and started the quick walk to the stables. Unfortunately, his talks with his favorite horses didn't help his melancholy mood. And of course, the animals didn't have any answers for him for how to deal with his growing feelings for Meg or his lingering guilt over Caroline.

"YOU WANT HER TO STAY?" Eli was sure Meg had been possessed by a different spirit. "Your mom?"

She wound her fingers around and around each other, her tell of her nerves. "She's just been...it's been kind of nice having her here. She's...different."

He supposed it didn't matter to him, other than he'd have his normal Meg back, and their normal life, and they could plan the New Year's Eve party together without the scrutiny of her mother.

"Have you talked to her about it?"

"Well, no."

"I think that's your first step."

"I can drive her myself," she said. "I know you're busy."

He wasn't busy but he didn't correct her. "I don't mind driving with you." It had been a fun trip for him, and he'd forever remember it as the time when he'd truly allowed himself to feel something for a woman other than Caroline.

"I guess I'll go find out then," she said. She walked away, her head held high, but Eli could sense her nerves hanging in the air. He prayed that her mother would be kind to her, the way she'd been on Christmas Day.

He watched her go and had just lifted his coffee mug to his lips when Stockton entered the room, his hair rumpled and still wearing his pajamas. "Hey, bud. Have you eaten breakfast?"

Celia hadn't been back since making all the holiday food, but Eli could pour a bowl of cereal for his son.

"No." Stockton yawned as he climbed up on the barstool. "Dad, Bailey says Meg's gonna be my mom. Is that true?"

Eli choked on the mouthful of coffee he'd just taken, the hot liquid leaking out of the corner of his mouth. He hurried to the sink and grabbed a towel, buying himself a few seconds to think of an answer.

When he faced his son again, Stockton just looked at him with mild puzzlement in his gaze.

"Why does Bailey think that?"

"She said you and Meg are dating. Like how her mom and Uncle Graham did before they got married."

Eli blinked, unsure of when seven-year-olds knew

about dating and marriage, though he supposed Bailey was unique in that regard. She had lived through her mom dating and getting remarried.

"I don't know, bud," Graham said slowly. "Meg and I... well, me and Meg...." He let his voice trail off, desperately wishing she were there. She'd know exactly what to say to him, how to reassure him, and how to classify their relationship.

"We like each other, right?" Eli tried again. "So I guess that's what people do when they're dating. They decide *how much* they like each other, and if it's a lot—like they fall in love—they get married."

"But you already like Meg a lot," Stockton said. "She's been livin' with us for a long time." His face scrunched up. "Right?"

"It's her job to live with us," Eli said carefully. "I pay her to take care of you, Stocky. She's your nanny."

Stockton cocked his head to the side. "I like her a lot."

"She loves you."

"I love her, too."

Eli wished his feelings were as simple as six-year-old emotions. "I like her a lot too, bud. We're...seeing how much we like each other. It's not a fast process." He got down a bowl and pulled out a box of the sugary flakes his son liked. "So it's not like we'll be getting married anytime soon or anything." He cut a look at Stockton. "Okay?"

"But if you do get married, will she be my mom?"

Eli poured milk on the cereal and sat beside his son at

the bar, a spoon extended to him. "She's not your mom, Stockton. But...she loves you and she takes care of you, and if we decide to get married, she'd be your step-mom. Like Uncle Graham is Bailey's step-dad. He's not her real dad."

Stockton took an overly large bite of his cereal, the question and answer session apparently over.

"But I love her like she's my daughter."

Eli startled at the introduction of Graham's voice to this conversation. "When did you get here?"

"Just now." He flashed a dark look at Eli and sat on the other side of Stockton. "I might not be Bailey's *biological* father, but I'm her *real dad.*" He glared at Eli over the boy's head and said, "It's cereal for breakfast?" He stood and went into the kitchen. "I know where Celia hides the good stuff." He reached up to a cabinet above the stove and pulled down a box of cereal that was basically miniature chocolate chip cookies.

"Hey!" Stockton pushed his sugary cereal away. "I want that too."

"Thanks, Uncle Graham," Eli said, his brother's words rolling around inside his mind. So maybe Eli had misspoken. He honestly had no idea how to navigate his relationship with Meg when it came to Stockton.

He did not want cookies for breakfast, so he kept sipping his coffee while Graham told Stockton about a new stray cat Bailey had found last night.

"Can I come see it?" Stockton abandoned another

bowl of cereal, and Eli thought it was a darn good thing they weren't hurting for money.

"I thought I was taking you down to the ranch today." Graham straightened his cowboy hat and looked at Eli. "Aren't you takin' Meg's mother home?"

"We were," Eli started, only to be interrupted by Meg.

"We still are."

He turned to find her standing in the doorway, her eyes flashing dangerously and glassy with tears at the same time. "Eli, will you please come help with the luggage?" She spoke in an even voice, but she spun on her heel and marched away before he could answer.

"Yep, let's go, bud." Graham herded Stockton toward the mudroom to get his coat and boots and gloves. He paused beside Eli. "Mom's coming to get him tonight. Good luck with everything." He clapped Eli on the shoulder and went to help Stockton.

Eli left his coffee mug beside the two half-eaten bowls of cereal, his main focus already back on Meg. Annoyance soared through him as he rounded the corner and entered the bedroom where her mother had stayed to find Meg folding the clothes and packing them.

"You're ready to head back, huh?" He leaned in the doorway and tried not to shoot lasers at Janice.

"Yes, yes," she said, patting her half-flat hair. "I have a hair appointment tomorrow, and Carrie's bringing pizza for Roland's birthday."

Eli had no idea who Roland was, but Carrie was Meg's

sister. So he just nodded like her reasons for needing to get home were completely valid.

"Hair appointments can be rescheduled," Meg said, not bothering to hide her frustration or keep her voice down. "And you can order pizza twenty-four hours a day, seven days a week. But whatever." She practically threw a shirt into the suitcase, where all the careful folding she'd done sort of got blown up.

"I don't like it all that much here," Janice said without any tact at all. "It's too close to Yellowstone. You know that place is going to blow up any day now, right?" She looked at Eli and then Meg, but Eli had no idea what to say. "This place will be wiped right off the map."

Meg zipped the bag shut and indicated it. "I'll go throw a few things in a bag, and we can go." She marched out of the room, and Eli was left with Janice, a lot of choice words flowing through his mind.

"Do you love your daughter?" he asked, pure curiosity in his voice.

Her mother looked at him with those same sharp eyes that had kept her undefeated in cribbage. "Of course I do."

"Maybe start treating her a little nicer, then." Eli picked up the suitcase and turned to leave. "We went *way* out of our way to get you here and she just wanted you to stay for a few extra days." The woman hadn't even been in town for forty-eight hours yet. "And you just put a hair appointment above her."

He looked back at her, and he was quite certain not

many people had spoken to her the way he just had. "Just something to think about." He set her suitcase outside his bedroom and hurried inside to pack his own bag, the excitement of another road trip with Meg building inside him.

TWELVE

TENSION FILLED the drive back to Boulder, no matter that Eli kept the cab filled with easy chatter and loads of country music. Meg couldn't force herself to participate, and the high of the eight-hour drive was when her mother fell asleep just past Cheyenne.

Eli fell silent then too, his right hand draped lazily over the steering wheel and his gaze steadfastly on the highway in front of him. Which, honestly, was fine with Meg. Her emotions zoomed just below the surface of her skin, and she didn't trust herself to keep them in check.

Her mom woke before they pulled into her driveway, which was completely shoveled and salted. Meg got out of the truck and stared at the cleared cement. "What happened here?"

Eli joined her near the front of the truck. "I paid for snow removal." He moved around her and helped her mom from the truck. His kindness knew no limits, and tears pricked Meg's eyes.

"Mom, Eli got you a snow removal service," she said brightly, as if she were talking to one of the children she nannied. "Isn't that great?"

Her mom looked at the ground as if just now noticing the three feet of snow wasn't there. "Thank you, Eli," she said tightly. She pressed her lips into a tight line and went with him toward the front door and up the steps. He'd somehow retrieved her bag when Meg wasn't looking, and she brought up the rear like a kicked puppy.

Eli opened the door and held it for her mom and her. He leaned in closer as she passed, a small, silent gesture that set Meg's heart to racing. "I got a maid service too," he said. "Looks like they've been here. They should come once a week."

"A maid service?" Her mom's voice pitched up on the last word. "They better not take anything."

Meg suppressed the snort that sprang to the back of her throat. As if her mother had anything worth taking. "I'm sure they won't, Mom."

"This is the best service in Boulder," he said. "I did my research." He set her bag at the mouth of the hall and glanced around.

Meg couldn't believe how clean the house was. The floors were actually gleaming, and she basked in what Eli's money could buy.

"They'll take your laundry, if you'd like," he said.

"And they do almost everything." He tapped the counter where a brochure had been left. "You can schedule them to come more often if you'd like. Get online here and choose the day you want. Everything's in here."

Her mom looked at the folder and then out the window, which Meg could actually see through now. The backyard was filled with snow, but it didn't matter. Meg could see it. She turned to Eli, her own gratitude almost overflowing.

"What a great Christmas present," she said, wanting to wrap her arms around his strong torso and smile at him until he kissed her.

"Yes, thank you." Her mom exhaled heavily as she sank into her beloved recliner. "And thanks for having me up to your family's lodge."

Meg noticed that all of her mom's thanks were going to Eli, as if Meg herself had done nothing, sacrificed nothing, endured *nothing*.

"Well, we can't stay," Eli said, finally a cool note in his voice. "My son needs us back at the lodge."

Surprise shot through Meg. Returning to Whiskey Mountain Lodge today hadn't been on their agenda. She met Eli's eyes and something unsaid passed between them, exactly like that time when Meg had wanted to stop and get Stockton an ice cream cone. Eli had gone along with her then, as if that whole outing had been planned.

"Right," Meg said. "He doesn't like it when we're gone."

Meg's mom looked back and forth between Eli and Meg. "You two talk about him like he belongs to you both."

"He does," Eli said, slinging his arm around Meg's waist. "I'm dating your daughter, Janice. And she's taken care of Stockton for four years—more than half of his life."

Pride and satisfaction rose through Meg, though she'd always been taught to suppress such feelings of self-importance. But Eli had claimed her. Just outright tucked her into his body and called her his. And said that Stockton was hers too.

Warmth flowed through her as if someone had put a blanket fresh from the dryer over her, and she watched her mother, almost daring her to say something.

"You make a nice couple," she finally said. "Thank you for driving me home." She made the hardest of tasks seem like nothing, and Meg felt her good feelings seeping away.

"Well, we should go." She stepped over to her mom and placed a kiss on her forehead. "It was good to see you, Mom. Fun playing cribbage." She walked to the front door and opened it again, unwilling to stay in her childhood home for much longer.

When she looked back, Eli was bent over her mother as well, whispering. Neither of them smiled as he stood, and he joined her at the door with a final, "Good-bye, Janice," before nudging Meg out the door and onto the porch.

She didn't dare speak until they were behind the

closed doors of the truck, with a few blocks of distance between them and her mom's house.

"What was that?" she asked. "What did you say to her? And where are we staying tonight?" Because she knew Eli didn't have the energy to drive another eight hours. Heck, she hadn't even been behind the wheel and she didn't have the energy to stay in this truck for much longer.

"I didn't want you staying with her," he said matter-of-factly, like it was his decision. "We'll find a hotel. You want to stay here, or drive to Cheyenne?"

"Here," Meg said wearily. "And I'd really like something with a lot of carbs to eat."

Eli chuckled. "So the 'I'm not hungry; let's just grab something at the gas station' thing was a ruse."

"Total ruse," she said, her stomach growling as a punctuation mark. "I didn't want to spend much more time with her." Her feelings rose, and she twisted toward him. "I just don't get her. We had *fun* playing cribbage. She seemed to have a good time with your brothers and your mom. But she can't stay for a few more days? What's she got here that's so important?"

The hurt leaked into her voice, and Meg shook her head before Eli could answer. "It's fine. Doesn't matter. It just...sucks."

Eli reached for her, a clear invitation for her to slide over and share his personal space, take from his comfort.

So she did, cozying right up to him and laying her head against his bicep.

"I'm so sorry, sweetheart." He pressed his lips to her temple, and Meg closed her eyes as a measure of peace drifted through her.

"At least I have you," she murmured. "And Stockton. I don't need her."

"Sure, you do," he said. "And it's okay to need her. You're ten times the mother she is." He looked at her, but she couldn't meet his eyes. "It's kind of like how I can't let go of Caroline."

Meg sucked in a breath, the sound sharp and painful in her ears and down her throat. Eli either noticed and didn't know what to say next or didn't want to acknowledge the depth of what he'd just said, or he hadn't noticed, because he kept quiet.

He drove for another few minutes and turned into a swanky hotel in downtown Boulder. "This is where I stayed a few nights ago. It was nice enough. Okay?"

She again averted her eyes as she slid across the seat and collected her purse. She nodded instead of speaking and opened her door to get out.

Eli took care of everything, because Eli had money. And emotions of steel. And loving kindness Meg could only pray for. So she let him take care of her, getting her a room with a Jacuzzi tub and ordering her favorite pizza—supreme—from the shop down the street. He claimed to be weary to the bone and said he'd text her later and maybe they could go to a movie. Then he disappeared into the room across the hall from hers, and Meg latched her door and leaned against it.

She wanted to cry, but the tears wouldn't come. Eli had never said what he'd whispered to her mother, and Meg honestly wasn't sure if she needed to know. What she did need to know was how Eli felt about her.

Her.

Not how he viewed her as Stockton's caregiver. She already knew that.

As she filled the Jacuzzi with scented bubbles and relaxing, rejuvenating oils, she wondered if Eli had ever considered her for the role his wife used to play. More than a mother. More than someone who made lunches and tucked little boys into bed.

But as someone who came to *his* bed, and supported *his* dreams, and stood by *his* side. As she soaked and let the stress of the morning and the drive melt out of her muscles, she determined that their relationship couldn't move forward until she talked to him about being his lover, his companion, his new wife.

SHE FOUND Eli sitting on the couch in the posh lobby, his head bent toward his phone and a happy little smile on his face as his thumbs flew over the screen. Meg took a moment to memorize him like that—carefree, handsome, happy. He was probably talking to Stockton, who used Graham's phone to communicate with Eli when he was out of town.

Or, if Meg was with Stockton, he used her phone.

Meg's heart squeezed with love for the little boy—and his father, and she knew in that moment that she'd fallen all the way in love with Eli Whittaker. Sure, her crush had some solid legs, but watching him care for her mother and interact with her even when she was a complete monster had solidified Meg's feelings for her boss.

Oh, boy. Her *boss*.

What if he didn't feel the same? What if he could never get past Caroline? Meg would lose everything—her heart, her home, the little boy she'd taken care of for so long.

Her heart pumped faster with fear now, and she tucked her hair nervously behind her ear, then flipped it back out. She didn't like how she looked with the A-line tucked behind her ears, and she'd worked hard with the straightener to get her long, front pieces to hang right.

She approached Eli, so many conversation topics teeming on the tip of her tongue. "Hey, handsome," she said in her best flirty voice.

He looked up from his phone, his closed-mouth smile bursting into one with teeth. He laughed and said, "Hey, yourself, pretty girl." He leaned toward her as if kissing was absolutely normal, and Meg supposed at this point, it was.

She kissed him and said, "Are you ready? I think the movie starts in twenty minutes, and I want popcorn."

"Yeah." He stood and tucked his phone in his back pocket. "Just chatting with Stocky. He's convinced Graham's going to get him a dog for his birthday this summer."

Meg shook her head. "I'll start talking to him about it once the new year hits."

"Good idea." Eli took her hand in his and they walked toward the exit. He used his free hand to press his cowboy hat more firmly on his head, and said, "I was wondering how set on seeing this movie you are."

She stepped outside, almost getting blown away by the wind. She cowered behind his body as she said, "I don't care. What else did you have in mind?"

"Just dinner," he said. "I mean, I know you had that carbo-loaded lunch a couple of hours ago, but I just want to...chill. Talk. Look at you." He smiled down at her, and she wondered if he could fall in love with her.

Her.

Not her as Stockton's nanny. But Meg the person. The woman who couldn't have children. The woman who had a broken relationship with both of her parents and her sisters. The woman who put everyone above herself.....

"Talking sounds nice," she said.

"I asked the concierge for a quiet restaurant," he said. "Where we could stay as long as we want. He gave me a few ideas."

Quiet sounded nice. "Lead on, Mister Whittaker." She grinned at him while his phone chimed.

He pulled out his phone and said, "Our ride is three minutes away."

"Oh, so it's not close."

"It's on the other side of town," he said. "Since you had pizza for lunch, I thought we'd do something different for dinner."

"So what kind of restaurant is it?"

"It's called Small," he said. "They have small plates of lots of different things. Appetizers mostly. One bites. That kind of stuff."

Meg considered him, trying to find any hint of a joke. She couldn't. "Sounds like a place you'd hate."

He kneaded her closer and put his arm around her, erasing the chill from the wind. "Yeah, but it's exactly what you'd like."

Her entire body seemed to buzz, and she knew she was going to say a lot tonight she wouldn't be able to take back. Starting with, "Eli, you keep saying and doing all the right things, and I'm going to fall right in love with you."

His mouth dropped open, and thankfully, Meg didn't have to explain anything because a black sedan pulled up to the doors and a man leapt out. "Eli Whittaker?"

Eli blinked at Meg one more time and then turned to the driver. "Yes."

"Where to?" he asked, indicating the logo of the same name on his car.

Eli seemed to have lost his cognitive functions, because he just stood there. Meg giggled and pulled him out of the safety of the door and into the wind.

"We're going to Small," she said. "I guess it's this restaurant on the other side of town."

"I know it," the man said, extending his hand for her to shake. "I'm your driver, Terrance, and I'll take you wherever you want to go." He opened the back door, and Meg ducked into the car, appreciating the scent of oranges and the black leather seats.

With Eli beside her and Terrance walking around the front of the car to get in the driver's seat, she said, "In fact, I might already be in love with you."

Eli choked, and Terrance opened the door, slid behind the wheel, and started the ignition. Classical music filled the car, and Meg added one more thing to her list of Things Eli Excelled At: Hiring a classy car service for a special date.

Seriously, there wasn't much the man couldn't do.

Except get over his first wife and see a future for himself, she thought, turning away from him and watching the lights of Boulder pass while Terrance tried to engage one of them in conversation.

THIRTEEN

I MIGHT ALREADY BE in love with you.

The words gonged through Eli's head on the way across town. Meg didn't say anything else, simply cuddled into him like she truly loved him. Memories he rarely let out of the box in the back of his mind streamed through his head.

He'd held Caroline like this once. When they lived in California, before Stockton was born, and he hadn't put a diamond on her finger yet. He'd felt just as unsettled then, as he'd known he was in love with her but he hadn't told her yet.

Was he in love with Meg too?

He looked out his window, the darkness blurring by a mirror to his muddied thoughts. The Where To? driver pulled up the restaurant, and Eli paid him before getting out of the sedan. He extended his hand for Meg, and kept her hand in his as they made their way inside.

The atmosphere was darker, the only lamps small orange candles on the tables. It was quiet, and only a few people sat in the booths. It was perfect. He remained quiet until he and Meg were seated across from each other, and then he looked her in the eye.

She seemed expectant, like he'd suggested they could talk, and well, she wanted him to start. But she'd already begun. And ended it with "I might already be in love with you."

He opened his mouth to say something, but nothing came out. The waiter appeared and he managed to order a drink just fine. So it was verbalizing his thoughts he couldn't do.

No, not his thoughts. His feelings—which was ten times harder than he'd thought it would be. He searched that open memory box for how he'd done such hard things with Caroline, and he realized that everything with her had been comfortable. After their wedding, they'd shared everything and he didn't worry about what she thought of him.

But that was what kept him mute now. He didn't want to disappoint Meg. Hurt her feelings. Or have her think badly of him.

"Eli." She placed her hands on the table in front of her, perfectly still. So calm, where he was usually the cool, collected one. "I'm wondering if you've thought of me as more than Stockton's nanny."

He scoffed, as if the question was ridiculous. "Of course I have."

"Have you?" She cocked her head. "Since we moved to Wyoming, you haven't had me read a single proposal. Or help with any of your work."

"I haven't done much work," he said. "You know that." His defenses were on high, and he tried to take the emotion out of his voice.

"How do you think of me?" she asked. "And you can't use 'nanny,' 'mother,' 'Stockton,' or 'friend.'"

Eli stared at her, trying to figure out what she wanted to hear so he could say it. "Meg," he started. "I think of you as...." He couldn't finish the sentence, not without the four words she'd said he couldn't use.

A frown pulled at her eyebrows and she reached for her soda as soon as the waiter set it down. She took several long swallows and then met his eye again. "I wish you'd use words like 'girlfriend,' or 'the woman who keeps me up at night,' or 'lover.'" She swallowed, her eyes bright in the soft light. Eli didn't like that, and something twisted in his chest.

"Meg, I do think of you like that."

She shook her head. "No, you don't." She picked up the menu and hid behind it. "But you should probably start. I could be your companion, Eli. Your lover. Your son's mother, sure. But what am I to you?" She lowered the menu just enough to peer over the top of it. "I could be your new wife." Her voice shook on the last word, and she promptly disappeared behind the laminated paper again.

Wife.

"You can't like me just because of Stockton. Not anymore."

"I don't—"

"I think I'll have the Six Sampler," she said over him, which only added fuel to Eli's frustrated fire. So she could talk when she wanted, but he couldn't?

Caroline, he thought. Because he hadn't given much thought to the actual romantic roles Meg could—and should—play in his life. He was attracted to her. He really enjoyed kissing her. But he'd never moved her into the role Caroline had played, and now Meg knew it.

They ordered, and without the menu, Meg made small talk with him. But it wasn't the kind of small Eli had pictured when coming to this restaurant. Problem was, he couldn't think of anything important to talk about except the elephant in the booth with them.

Dinner was short, and not as peaceful as Eli would've liked. They returned to the hotel and went up to the sixth floor together. He paused outside her door, so many insecurities racing through him.

He finally told himself to be brave for thirty seconds and *talk to her.* He faced her and took both of her hands in his. "Meg, when I think of you, I think of a beautiful, capable woman who makes my heart race."

He swallowed, his throat so dry. "I think it might take a bit of time for me to think of you beyond Stockton, but I'd really like it if you'd give me the chance."

A few seconds passed while she considered him. Then she smiled and said, "All right, Eli."

A smile sprang to his face. "Yeah?"

"Yeah." She pressed a chaste kiss to his lips. "Just as long as you start *looking* at me."

Eli blinked at her, unsure of what she meant. "I am looking at you."

She didn't say anything, but this time when she kissed him, it was much slower, with much more passion, and much less chaste.

ELI MADE lists and checked things off of them, spending long hours at his desk as he made all the arrangements for the New Year's Eve party he was putting together at the lodge. They'd have four guests taking up their six rooms upstairs, and he wanted to provide the "party of the century" as he'd promised.

He often found himself staring at the wall in front of him as he thought about Meg. Thought about waking up next to her. Thought about sharing his deepest fears with her. Thought about leaning on her for comfort and help when he was feeling low.

She'd been right—she could be so much more to Eli

than simply Stockton's mother. Her role as Eli's wife would be just as vital to him as Caroline had been.

About that time in his thoughts, the fear took over. As one day passed and then two, and finally three, he'd separated the reasons for his fear into two categories. One, he was still terrified of replacing Caroline. She'd been one of a kind, and Eli still felt a measure of disloyalty whenever he thought about marrying Meg.

Two, Caroline had been taken from him so suddenly and so soon. And he had a little bit of fear that Meg would be taken too.

No matter what, he'd thought long and hard about what she'd said. He didn't want to be the guy that fell for her because she took good care of his son and was conveniently located just down the hall.

But at the moment...he was exactly that guy.

He hung his head, his checklist forgotten.

"Hey." Graham stuck his head into the office. "The Lawson family is here, and they want the rundown for tomorrow night."

Eli stood and smoothed down his suit before buttoning the jacket. "Thanks, Graham." He tried to push away his troubling thoughts of Meg, but they wouldn't go far.

Graham didn't move out of the doorway. He looked at Eli with his older brother eyes though they stood at the same height now. "You okay?"

"I'm fine," Eli said.

"You've seemed...off since you got back from Colorado."

"Meg said...." Eli exhaled harshly. "It's a long story. I don't have time to tell it." He turned back to his desk and picked up a blue folder which held the Lawson's itinerary and all the details they'd need for the shindig tomorrow night.

Graham hadn't budged when Eli turned around again. "I'll be here when you're done," he said. "I want to hear all about what Meg said."

Eli glared at his brother. "When did you become so nosy?"

"About the time I saw my brother wallowing in misery."

"I'm not miserable. Or wallowing."

"Do you know how many times you've sighed over the past three days?"

"I have no idea." Eli rolled his eyes and flapped the folder. "Can you move, please?"

Graham stepped into the office, leaving the doorway open. "I'll be right here."

Eli said, "You do that," wondering if Graham's words were a threat or a promise. Didn't matter. He needed to meet with the Lawson's and then he could figure out how to explain his situation with Meg when he didn't understand it himself.

THE WALLS of Whiskey Mountain Lodge vibrated with the loud music coming through the built-in stereo surround sound speakers. The New Year's Eve party was in full swing, with Beau playing DJ and taking requests from the guests and Eli making sure the tables stayed full of food and drinks.

The dinner, DJ, and dance party would end by nine, at which time, the guests would be moved into the basement for games or movies until the ball dropped. And, of course, there would be an endless supply of chips and guacamole, as well as caramel popcorn. Eli had never rung in a new year without his favorite snacks, and Whiskey Mountain Lodge wouldn't be without them either.

Stockton came out of the kitchen carrying the six-pack of soda Eli had sent him to retrieve.

"Put it on the table, bud." Eli indicated the empty spot for the diet cola. The little boy did as instructed and then snatched one of his favorite fudge-striped cookies.

"Last one," Eli said, though he had no idea how he could police such a thing. There were bags and bags of cookies in the kitchen, and Stockton could take as many as he wanted while Eli was out here babysitting bowls of candy and bags of chips.

The guests seemed like they were having fun. Beau too. Andrew had gone down to their mother's to spend the evening with her as she'd been feeling under the weather and didn't want too loud of a party.

Laney and Graham had opted to stay home with

Bailey, and once Stockton went to bed, Meg would join the party as Eli's date. She hadn't said anything else about him looking at her, and the past few days had been business as normal between them.

She took care of Stockton during the day while Eli worked. And she was on-duty tonight too, at least until the boy went to bed. Eli wanted to share a kiss with her. One that testified of what kind of year they'd have together. Problem was, he wasn't sure what kind of kiss that would be.

Beau finished up with, "Thank you, folks! Happy New Year!" before looking at Eli. The music quieted and Beau spoke into the microphone again. "We'll be moving downstairs for games, pool, more food, and we'll be showing a movie in the theater room. You can cast votes for which flick you want on the board downstairs. So head on down there at your leisure and let's keep this party going!"

Eli was glad Beau had agreed to be the voice of this party. Normally, his youngest brother wore a three-piece suit and sat behind a desk while he studied cases. As the top lawyer in Coral Canyon, he did a lot of cases through Jackson County, which kept him plenty busy—and quite stuffy.

But not tonight, and Eli gave him a thumbs-up as several people passed the DJ table in favor of the steps leading into the basement. Meg and Stockton appeared to help Eli take the snacks downstairs, and he grabbed a bowl of cheese puffs so he wouldn't grab onto Meg and swing her around to the echo of the disco music.

Once everything was moved, and the guests were happy, with the movie playing, Meg took Stockton upstairs to put him to bed. Eli followed them for a few moments of reprieve before returning to the basement, and Beau gave his brother high-five as he zipped his leather jacket to his chin in preparation to leave.

"Careful on the bike," Eli said. "It's real dark out there."

"But it hasn't snowed for a couple of days," Beau said. "So the roads are dry." He grabbed his helmet from the kitchen counter and headed for the front door. Eli watched him go with a slip of envy needling him. Beau lived a fairly drama-free life. Drank coffee for breakfast. Had his secretary order in lunch. Worked through dinner.

Meg appeared in the arched doorway leading into the hall. "He wants you to come say goodnight."

Eli pushed away from the counter where he'd been standing and went to tuck his son in tight. The bathroom door was almost all the way closed, but let in a four-inch swath of light.

"Hey, bud." Eli bent down and gave his son a hug. "You go right to sleep, okay?" He gazed down into his son's eyes—so much like Caroline's. He pulled in a tight breath at the memory, glad he still had this piece of her.

For the first several months after her death, Stockton had reverted in a lot of ways. He couldn't sleep in his own bed. He'd just been potty trained and suddenly had forgotten how to use the toilet. He'd sucked his thumb for a while.

Eli had been equally as lost, but it had been Stockton who'd pulled him out of his funk, forced him to keep living, made him want to build a life for the two of them despite their loss.

Stockton wrapped his little arms around Eli's neck. "Night, Daddy. See you next year." He started giggling, and Eli couldn't help laughing with him.

"Did Meggy tell you that one?" he asked.

"No, Bailey. Meggy let me text her tonight." Stockton settled into his pillows.

"Well, it's a good one." He tucked the blanket in tight against Stockton's side. "Love you, Stocky."

"Love you too, Daddy."

Eli stepped out and pulled the door closed behind him before returning to the kitchen.

"Everything go okay?" Meg asked.

"Yep." Eli plucked a chocolate chip cookie from the store-bought bag. Meg made a face as he ate the whole thing in two bites. "What?"

"Those aren't real, you know that, right?"

"Oh, are these cookies not up to your standard?" It had taken Eli most of the morning to buy the food for this party, as a grocery store wasn't a place where he spent much time.

She shook her head. "Homemade only."

"Some of us take what we can get." He picked up another cookie and offered it to her before stuffing the whole thing in his mouth.

She laughed and swatted playfully at him. "Well, at least now I know you're not perfect."

That made Eli sober. "Meg." He shook his head. "Of course I'm not perfect."

She lifted one shoulder into a shrug, and asked, "Are we going downstairs to the party? I've just been listening to it behind this wall. I'd kinda like to join it."

He smiled, though it didn't come easily to him. She thought him to be perfect? He couldn't live up to that. No one could. "Lead us down, sweetheart."

Meg gave him a flirtatious smile and turned toward the steps that went into the basement. He followed her, his nerves already fraying though midnight was still three hours away.

FOURTEEN

MEG DIDN'T WANT to play games—not the board kind laid out on the table where two couples were currently laughing, and not the relationship kind where she kept tiptoeing around Eli.

She'd spent a long time on her knees the night before, praying and begging God to guide her when it came to her boss, Stockton's dad, and the man she knew she loved. Eli had asked for more time to see her with different eyes, but Meg wasn't sure he truly needed it. After all, she'd been right in front of him for four years.

And she didn't want to start a new year differently than how she'd end it. Not again. She wasn't a child anymore, and if Eli couldn't open his eyes and see her standing there, her arms and heart open to him and Stockton, she needed to move on.

She still had time to find someone else, maybe go

through the adoption process or fostering program to build a family.

So she pointed to the theater room and said, "You want to watch the movie?"

Eli turned his attention from the hot tub, where another couple had decided to take their New Year's party, and smiled. "Sure, a movie's fine."

The brilliance of his smile nearly knocked Meg over, and she wondered if she'd ever be able to move on if their relationship ended. A tremor of terror shook her legs, but she managed to walk to the door and push it open.

The family staying at the lodge and the last couple had chosen the movie, so the theater was fairly empty. She kept going straight and moved down the back row to the far wall. Out of sight. Maybe she'd be able to talk to Eli here. Whisper her love for him and beg him to say it back.

Don't do that, she told herself as she sat in the luxury recliner. Eli lifted the armrest between them and sat beside her, waiting for her to snuggle into his side before he put his arm around her and lifted his leg rest.

They watched a few minutes of the movie, Meg's anxiety playing leapfrog with itself until she was so nervous she couldn't concentrate.

Eli pressed his lips to her temple and said, "What's wrong?"

She lifted herself up to look at him, and the light from the movie played over his handsome features, illuminating concern and compassion.

I love you.

I love you.

I'm in love with you.

She couldn't make the words come out of her mouth. So she kissed him instead, hoping the emotion would translate equally as well. Eli kissed her back, and surely the spark there, the slow, careful way he stroked his mouth against hers indicated he had strong feelings for her too. Right?

Maybe that's enough, she thought. But she knew it wasn't. She didn't want him to like her because of how she took care of his son. She *had* to be more than that to him. It was non-negotiable.

"Hey," he whispered, pulling back. "You're not okay."

The fact that he knew, could feel it, made her heart feel like bursting. She shook her head. "I'm not okay."

"What's wrong?"

She looked into his eyes, the hazel-ness of them swallowed up in the darkness. "I'm...I love you, Eli."

He smiled. "And that's not okay?"

He didn't say it back, and Meg's pulse pounced against her ribs. "It's...how do you feel about me?"

She wasn't blind, and something on the movie exploded, providing plenty of light to see the indecision in his eyes.

"I need to know," she pressed him. "I...this year...I can't keep wasting time."

He narrowed his eyes. "Do you think that's what you're doing here? Wasting time?"

"I want a family," she said, her bravery settling into place. "And if it's not going to be with you and Stockton, I need to move on." There. She'd said it. She'd spent so much of her childhood saying nothing, and she couldn't keep doing it. Not with Eli. Not anymore.

"I want to start this year off right," she continued. "And...I just need to know if you're going to be in it or not."

"A year's a long time, Meg."

"It is." And it would probably take her that long to recover from her broken heart. Because Eli wasn't saying or doing any of the things Meg had imagined he might. Her stupid fantasies. They'd never gotten her into quite this much trouble, but over the past four days, she'd thought Eli would at least be able to promise her *some*thing.

"Meg, I'm going to be real honest here." He ran one hand down the side of her face. "I like you, but this is too fast for me. I need...I'm not ready to say what you want me to say. I'm not ready to tell you this year will be exactly what you want it to be. It's too much, too soon, too...." He trailed off, a measure of agony glinting in his eyes now.

Meg recoiled from the truth in his words, the desperation in his tone. "How long do you need?" She'd suffered hardships in her life too. It had taken her a while to come to terms with the fact that she would never be pregnant, never carry a child, never be a biological mother. But not four years. It hadn't taken her *four years* to think past her own trauma and try to find a new future. A happier future. A hopeful future.

"I can't answer that," he said. "I know you want me to. I know you—"

"I think you've had enough time." Meg stood and stepped past him, her muscles firing on all cylinders and her heart wailing inside her chest.

"Meg."

She kept going, needing to get away from the tantalizing scent of his skin. She licked her lips and found the taste of him there, and tears sprang to her eyes. Her whole life had been wrapped up in him and his son for so long.

"Not anymore," she whispered furiously to herself as she heaved open the big door and burst back out into the game room. No one even glanced her way. Of course they wouldn't. The three couples in the vicinity were happily in love, away on a New Year's vacation to ring in the next twelve months that they'd spend merrily together.

Meg had never considered herself a bitter person, and she'd had some reasons to be. But all she felt pouring through her, coating her throat, her tongue, her mouth, was pure bitterness. She'd taken one step when Eli's fingers wrapped around her forearm.

"Meg," he said again. "Don't go."

She turned to face him, take one long last look at his handsome features, those eyes she'd fallen in love with first, that beard that called to her, his strong jaw and mouth.

"I quit," she said. "Good-bye, Eli." She pulled her arm out of his grip and started up the steps, her adrenaline fueling her enough to take them two at a time. She expected him to come thundering after her, demand she stay until he found a new nanny, maybe even apologize and confess his love for her.

Another stupid fantasy, she thought when she reached the top of the stairs and there was no sound or activity following her. Spurred by the silence, she ran down the hall and into her bedroom.

Tears flowed down her face as she punched the lock and started packing. She called a car service, not even hearing how much it would cost on New Year's Eve to come get her and take her to a hotel.

It didn't matter. She couldn't stay under this roof, with Eli so close, for another night. So close, and yet so far away. Time passed, and Meg hated that everything she owned could fit into two suitcases. But she didn't have furniture. Bedding. Kitchenware. She had clothes and a few knick knacks she'd picked up in the places she'd worked.

Time passed, and she calmed, and when her phone chimed that the car she'd booked would be arriving in five minutes, she tiptoed through the shared bathroom and into Stockton's room.

The little boy looked like an angel as he slept. She

brushed his hair off his forehead and placed a kiss there. "Stocky," she whispered and his eyes fluttered open. "Hey, bud." The emotion in her voice wasn't lost on her. She'd said good-bye to several children over the years, and each one was emotional and difficult.

"Hey, Meggy." His voice sounded froggy and thick.

"Hey." She didn't bother trying to wipe or hide her tears. "I have to leave, Stocky. Okay? But I didn't want to go without saying good-bye."

He sat up. "You're leaving? When will you be back?"

She shook her head and pulled the little boy into a hug. "I'm not coming back, bud." She released him and tucked the blanket around him absently. "You be good for your daddy, okay? And always remember that I love you." She closed her eyes and pressed her forehead to Stockton's. "You're my favorite boy," she said as her phone went off again. Her ride was here. She needed to go. "I love you."

She straightened and backed up a step before turning to leave.

"Meggy," he said, but she kept going. Back in her room, she gathered her two suitcases and squared her shoulders. In the hall, Stockton stood in his doorway and Eli stood in his.

"Thank you for having me," she said. "You can send my last payment as usual."

"Meg," Eli said, and as she approached, she found

evidence that the big, burly, billionaire cowboy had been doing some crying of his own.

"Daddy, why's Meggy leaving?" Stockton darted across the hall and Eli tucked him into his side.

"I don't know, bud."

That made Meg pause, and when she was almost past him too. She twisted back and said, "You broke my heart, Eli Whittaker. That's why I'm leaving." She hurried now, down the hall and through the foyer and out the front door.

The car waited, exhaust lifting from the back bumper. A man got out and helped her put her bags in the trunk, and when she was safely in the warm backseat, he said, "Where to?"

Eli had paid her well over the years, and Meg had enough money to go somewhere to start fresh. Somewhere warm, she decided as she'd really liked her time in Bora Bora.

"Just the hotel in town," she said. And after that, she'd head for the west coast, knowing if Eli couldn't get past Caroline, he'd never come to California to look for Meg.

FIFTEEN

ELI WATCHED the cheering people on the big screen, counting down as the year ended and a new one began. The ball dropped, and the couples in the theater kissed. Eli stared at them with blind eyes, his own New Year's kiss with Meg a dot on some distant horizon.

She'd left.

Left Whiskey Mountain Lodge.

Left Stockton.

Left him.

His heart felt like someone had encased it in cement and then tried to put it back in his chest. It couldn't beat against the confines, and his ribs were too weak to hold the organ in place.

At least the party was over. People stayed up for a few more minutes, finishing their games and collecting their stuff. Then everyone went upstairs, leaving Eli in the basement to clean up.

But he wasn't about to do that. Annie would come tomorrow and take care of all of it. He'd pay her whatever she asked, because at this moment, all he had left was money in the bank. Money in the bank that couldn't buy him what he wanted—which was Meg.

He turned away from the cups and bowls of snacks. "Why couldn't you say something then?" he asked himself, an angry note in his voice. She'd been saying so much, and asking so many hard questions, and Eli simply didn't have the answers.

What he had said—that this was too fast, too soon, too new—that was all true. But how could he expect Meg to just hang around while he figured things out? Things he hadn't even known he needed to figure out.

His boots rang angrily on the tile at the top of the stairs as he stomped down the hall to his bedroom. He'd tucked Stockton into his huge king-sized bed after the boy had started to cry that Meg had left.

Eli had shed a tear or two himself, but not in front of his son. He hadn't allowed himself to do that when Caroline died, and he wouldn't now. Alone, maybe. In the shower, sure. All the evidence washed down the drain.

But as he closed the door behind him and listened to the soft breathing of his son, his tears came anyway. "What do I do now?" he pleaded, casting his eyes toward the ceiling, toward God.

He hadn't been down to church in weeks, since the snow really made getting down to town difficult and sometimes dangerous.

Not only did he need a new nanny, but he needed someone to help him stitch his heart back together long enough to take a decent breath and take the next step.

He'd felt like this before. He knew how to do this.

He stepped toward the bed, intending to crawl in with Stockton and hold his son until morning. But he found himself falling to his knees instead.

"I've felt like this before," he said, his tears hot in his eyes. "When Caroline died. I loved her so much."

A sense of calmness descended over him and he wiped the tears from the corners of his eyes. His thoughts straightened and aligned, and he realized that he'd felt like this before because he'd loved his wife.

So that meant he loved Meg too.

"I already know I love her as a friend," he said, his voice only slightly pinched now. "As Stockton's nanny. But can I love her as a wife?"

Of course you can.

The thought entered his mind, spoken in Caroline's voice, something he hadn't heard in so, so long. He actually opened his eyes and looked around for her, expecting to see her standing there, telling him it was okay to love another woman, provide another mother for their son.

Of course, she wasn't there, and Eli's thoughts scattered again. "I'm sorry, Caroline," he whispered to the room where a piece of her still slept.

Several long moments passed where Eli felt like something that had been poisoning his soul for so long got plucked out. He'd never told anyone the reason he felt so guilty after Caroline's death, why he couldn't return to California, why he'd hired a nanny for Stockton and then moved somewhere tropical.

He'd hidden the feelings, boxed them up tight, even when Meg was there, trying to tug the tape off of them. He hadn't told her why he was still so hung up on Caroline either. But now, as the dark, cesspool of guilt emptied and he became free, he finally understood and knew.

And he'd have to tell Meg if he wanted her back.

HE DIDN'T MAKE the call in the morning. The lodge stayed quiet for hours, until near noon when the first guests came down to check out. Eli greeted them with freshly brushed teeth behind his plastic smile and said he hoped they'd come back next year.

He called Graham and asked if Stockton could come down to the ranch and play with Bailey, and his brother said yes. Eli knocked on the front door and then twisted the knob with a "Hello? It's Eli."

"C'mon in," Laney called from the general vicinity of the kitchen. "Bailey's not in from the barn yet. She and

Graham are...." Her voice trailed off as she came around the corner and saw Eli. "Oh, honey, what's wrong?" She looked at Stockton, who'd barely said two words to Eli that day.

"Nothing," Eli lied. "I just...Stockton's bored. Needs a playmate. I thought he...." Eli shrugged, not wanting to admit that being a chipper father when he felt like this was really hard.

"Sure, yeah." Laney wiped her hands on her apron. "I'm just making bagels for later." She reached her hand out. "Want to help me, Stockton?"

Stockton released Eli's hand and walked down the hall and took Laney's hand. "Stay there," she said before taking the boy into the kitchen and setting him to some task. Eli could hear her voice, but he didn't pay attention to the words. She'd come back and lecture him, and Eli deserved it. But he stayed, because Laney might be able to help him get Meg back.

Sure enough, only a few moments passed before Laney returned, coming all the way to the front door and speaking in a hushed tone. "What is going on? Both of you are acting like someone died."

"Meg left," Eli said simply, looking Laney right in the eyes.

"She left...left?"

"Left. As in, she quit, and she's not coming back."

Laney's eyes rounded and she frantically searched Eli's face. "What happened? She liked you so much."

"Yeah, well, that's what happened."

"Eli Whittaker." Laney folded her arms. "I've known you my whole life. Babysat you and everything. You've always been the brother everyone loved. Surely you know that."

Eli shrugged, unsure of whether what she said was true or not. "What are you getting at, Laney?"

"Did you hurt her?"

"I'm sure I did."

"What happened?"

Eli's throat narrowed and it was difficult to breathe, let alone swallow. "She told me she loved me, okay? And she kept asking me how I felt about her, and she wanted me to see her as more than Stockton's nanny, and it was...it was all just a lot to take in, you know? And I told her I needed time." His chest heaved as the emotion rolled from him.

"So you didn't say it back."

He shook his head.

"And she didn't want to give you more time."

"She said I'd had enough."

"And have you?"

"I couldn't let go of Caroline."

Laney softened just the teensiest bit. "Oh, Eli. Of course you can. You've had Meg in your life longer than you ever had Caroline. Why can't you let go of her?"

Eli just shook his head. Laney wasn't going to be the first person he spilled his secret to. "Any ideas for how to get her back?"

Laney just watched him for what seemed like the longest time. The backdoor opened and Graham said, "Hoo boy! It is cold out there," before closing the door with a bang.

"Maybe she needs some time," Laney said. "We'll keep Stockton as long as you want." She turned and headed back toward the kitchen just as Graham said, "Oh, Stocky's here. Where's Aunt Laney, bud?"

Eli slipped out the front door before his brother could see him standing in the hall. He didn't need to repeat himself.

And he didn't want to give Meg any more time to get away. She'd said she wanted to start this year off right, and that meant he had to contact her today.

HE CALLED her from the cab of his SUV, but she didn't answer. After the short, one-mile drive back to the lodge, Eli called her again. This time a man picked up the phone with an aged, "Hello?"

"Oh, um." Eli didn't know what to say. "I'm looking for Meg Palmer?"

"Meg Palmer," the old man bellowed. "Do we know a Meg Palmer?"

"This is her phone," Eli said, wondering who this was. "Who are you? It's Eli Whittaker."

"Oh, Eli." The man was practically shouting. "It's Eli

Whittaker." And he had an audience. "It's Redd Sugar-house. I just picked up this phone."

Redd Sugarhouse owned the coffee bar in town. So Meg had been there at some point. Scratching and scuffling came through the line and then a woman said, "Hello, Eli, dear. It's Maysie. I told Redd to mind his own business, but when a phone rings, he answers it."

Eli managed to crack a smile. "It's fine, Maysie. Do you know where the owner of the phone is?"

"We didn't even know who it belonged to. You want to come get it?"

"How long has it been there?"

"Oh, a while, hon."

A while. Which meant Meg could be hours and hours away by now, what with the slow morning and the way Eli had barely been able to get his son out of bed.

"I'll come get it," he said. Maybe he could determine where she'd gone by her calls or texts. He drove the twenty minutes into town, the radio off and his thoughts his only company. He pulled up to the coffee house, the parking lot full for mid-afternoon. He supposed a lot of people had gotten a slow start to the day.

He caught Maysie's eye as soon as he entered, the scent of dark roast a siren's call to him. "I'll take a deep brew," he said. "And that phone."

She passed him the device and rang up his order. He took his coffee to a corner table that was barely big enough for his mug and his own phone and swiped on Meg's.

She had a lock screen, but he knew the code. They'd trusted each other explicitly, and when Eli hadn't had anyone else, he'd always had Meg.

A moan started internally. Why hadn't he been able to *say something* last night? Something to keep her in his life just a little longer. Something to let her know that he loved her and wanted to be with her.

She hadn't made any calls this morning at all. Sent no texts. None that were still stored on the phone anyway. With his money, he could probably hire someone to find anything she'd deleted, but he wasn't sure he wanted to go down that road. It seemed dark, and twisty, and totally not like something he'd do to someone he loved.

She had called one number last night, and when Eli dialed it, he got a chipper man saying, "Anytime Ride, this is Daniel, when do you need a car?"

"I'm wondering if you can tell me about a job last night," Eli said, drawing out the last word.

"Are you a cop?"

"No, sir."

"We don't give out our client's information or where we took them," Daniel said. "Not without a warrant, anyway."

Since Eli didn't have one of those, he said, "Okay, thank you," and hung up.

The phone had held some measure of hope, but now that Eli hadn't been able to find anything on it, it only represented a piece of Meg he didn't know what to do with.

"Where are you?" he asked the picture of her and Stockton she'd saved as her background. It didn't answer, and Eli had no idea where a woman like Meg would go. No roots. No family she cared about. The whole world was wide open to her, and Eli hated himself for snapping the tether that had kept her in his life.

SIXTEEN

MEG FELT DIVIDED IN TWO. Right down the middle. Half of her felt freer than she had in years, with a wad of cash in her purse and the radio in the rental car on loud as she left the state of Wyoming in her rear view mirror.

The other half was equally as fearful, frustrated, and downright screaming at her to go back and make sure someone—*anyone*—knew where she was going and how to find her. After all, she could go right off the road on these lonely stretches of highway in Idaho and not a single person would even miss her.

The thought made her sad, and lonely, and she pushed it away. The last thing she needed was to worry about a car accident, and she readjusted her grip on the steering wheel.

She'd gotten as much cash as she could off her credit card that morning, as all the banks were closed for New

Year's Day. And she'd purposely left her phone in the coffee bar, knowing it wouldn't take Eli long to call.

In fact, she was a bit surprised she hadn't woken up to a half-dozen messages from him that morning. As soon as she could, she'd empty her bank account, because Eli had endless resources to track her movement with debit and credit cards, and she needed a clean break.

"You're making him seem like a stalker," she muttered to herself. And he wasn't a stalker. But Eli Whittaker also didn't hear no very often, and when he did, he knew how to turn it into a yes. Into another opportunity. It was actually one of the things she liked about him.

"You like everything about him." She'd been talking to herself for hours, but she saw no reason to stop. It wasn't like she had anyone to talk to, and her two suitcases in the back seat didn't care if she was the crazy lady who talked jibberish in the front seat.

And besides, she didn't like *everything* about him. She didn't like that he couldn't let go of the past. That he hadn't truly seen her all these years. That he was so indecisive and couldn't express his feelings.

Yeah, Eli had a few black marks against him, but being a stalker wasn't one of them.

She drove as long as she was emotionally and physically able, finally pulling into a hotel in Elko, Nevada. She paid cash for a room and hoped she could get to a bank in the morning and close this chapter on the first thirty-two years of her life.

"Time to move on," she announced to the empty room. She'd find a new job in California, and she'd make new friends, and she'd find a way to fit someone into the giant Eli-shaped hole in her heart.

Right now, that spot in her chest throbbed with an ache she didn't know how to soothe. So she got out her laptop and started looking at the maps. She wanted warm, Southern California, so her next destination was San Diego.

The computer told her it was another eleven hours from Elko, and Meg laid her head in her hands. She'd only driven for six and a half hours today, and she felt like she'd been churning under the wheels for some of that.

"We'll play it by ear," she said as if someone else was there to agree or disagree with her.

The following day, she didn't feel like stopping until she made it to the beach. So she drove, and drove, and drove, finally arriving at a hotel she thought she could afford by about seven p.m.

She checked in and dumped her carryon bag in the room before taking a quick walk between a couple of buildings and coming to the ocean. It spread out before her, and it was as if her heart grew wings and lifted from the soles of her feet where it had settled sometime last night.

The gravity of what she'd done hadn't hit her until after she'd eaten and showered and was lying on the hard, hotel bed, the TV flickering in the dark in front of her.

Then she'd really realized that she didn't have a single soul in the world to turn to. She'd written down Eli's number before leaving her phone behind, and she'd picked up a disposable cell in Jackson Hole. She wasn't stupid, and she knew she'd need a way to call for help if she got a flat tire as she drove to the beach.

But she hadn't had any problems, and now she stood with sand between her toes and the entire world before her.

"I can do this," she said, and the ocean waves simply repeated it back to her, already her biggest fans.

A WEEK LATER, Meg stood in front of the mirror in the hotel where she was still staying. She'd found an apartment, but it wouldn't be ready until the fifteenth, so she still had another week to call the Motel 8 her home.

She slicked her palms down the front of the new black skirt she'd bought over the weekend, for her new office job she'd gotten on Friday.

God had somehow made the stars align for her, and Meg had spent more and more time talking to Him lately. It was either the Lord or herself, and Meg liked feeling like someone else was out there listening.

"Okay, you're ready." She turned away from her reflection and headed outside. She'd decided to keep the rental car until she was settled into her new apartment, but she wouldn't need a vehicle after that. She'd be living right next to a bus stop, and she didn't want to burn through her savings too fast.

Everything in California seemed to cost more than Meg was used to, right down to a gallon of milk or a cup of coffee. But she still splurged on her morning to-go concoctions, and she'd finally found something about the lodge that could be improved: better morning coffee service.

If she'd asked Eli, he probably would've had someone come out and cater a pot just for her every morning.

The thought of Eli came so effortlessly into her mind, as they had been for a solid week. It stung, as usual, and Meg tried to hold onto it instead of push it away. She'd learned that she couldn't bottle up so many emotions and expect to find happiness.

So she let Eli linger in her thoughts as she went downstairs to her car and then down the street to her job. She'd gotten a secretary position in a busy law office, and she hadn't even had to give Eli as a reference. Something about them being desperate and her being able to type and start immediately.

So she stepped into Janklow, Nesbit, and Johnson, her purse clutched tightly to her side and her eyes scanning left and right, right and left.

She'd been hired by a man name Luke, she knew that, and his office had been...there. In the corner. She stepped that way, almost getting trampled by two women as they came out of a conference room with at least three feet of stacked folders between them.

"Oh, sorry." Meg fell back, realizing her "power skirt" held much less voltage than theirs.

"It's fine," one of them, a brunette who'd pulled her hair back into a severe ponytail, said. "You must be the new secretary." A smile touched her face, and Meg wondered how she held that stack of folders with her skinny arms.

"I'm Tia. Follow me."

"Okay."

Tia walked away, immediately turning her attention back to the other woman, also a brunette, but with streaks of blonde in her hair, which fell around her shoulders in magnificent waves. They both wore heels, and Meg's sandaled feet could barely keep up.

"This is June. She works for Luke too."

"June. Got it." Meg couldn't believe how busy this place was, and it was only nine o'clock in the morning.

"This is your desk," June said, pointing to one of a triad situated in front of three doors—one in the corner, and one on each adjoining wall. The doors were all open, and lights on, and men talked on phones. "You're Taylor's PA, and you probably have one minute until arrival." June settled at one of the desks while Tia placed her stack of folders beside the one June had already set down.

"I'm Lonnie's PA." Tia smiled. "And you'll come to

lunch with us today so we can talk about more than boring lawyer stuff."

Warmth spread through Meg that had nothing to do with the California sun that shone brilliantly beyond the windows. "Sounds good."

"Is this my new girl?"

Meg turned toward the feminine yet no-nonsense voice to find a blonde woman wearing a gray pair of slacks and a flowery blouse standing there. "I'm Taylor Janklow. You must be Meg. Meg? Yes, Meg. I think that's what Luke said."

"That's what he said." Meg stepped forward and shook Taylor's hand. She wasn't sure why Luke did Taylor's hiring for her, but Meg was exceedingly glad to be working for a woman. After all, she'd already endured falling for her boss once, and this way, she knew it wouldn't happen again.

"All right. I'll need you in my office for twenty minutes, and then I'll release you to June." She flashed a quick smile in June's direction. "Luke said he could spare you to train Meg."

"I'm already geared up for it, ma'am." June gave the fakest smile Meg had ever seen, but Taylor just turned and went into her office.

Meg stared at her back and then at June. "Taylor."

"Go on," June hissed. "She doesn't like to be kept waiting."

❄

IT SEEMED like a miracle that Meg made it through the week. She hadn't started a new job in a long, long time, and she'd never been a secretary before. She thought she'd faked it pretty well, and she really enjoyed having girl-friends.

"Hey, there." Tia slid into the front seat of Meg's car while June wrestled her giant beach bag into the back.

"Hey." Meg smiled at them, her heart only twitching a couple of times at the thought of leaving Laney and Celia behind in Wyoming without so much as a good-bye. A way to contact her. Nothing.

Well, Laney had already contacted her on social media, but the message had only said *I miss you. Please let me know you're okay.*

Laney had always been particularly sensitive about Eli, and Meg had responded with *I'm okay.*

Laney had immediately asked about Eli, and mentioned how miserable he was, and Meg had quickly signed off. Of course Eli was miserable. She'd been taking care of his every need for four years.

"This has been the longest week ever," June said as Meg pulled out of the parking lot. "I can't wait to just lie on the beach." She exhaled in a long hiss, and Meg caught her with her eyes closed when she looked in the rear-view mirror.

"Where are we going?" Meg asked. "You two forget I'm new here."

"Coronado," Tia said at the same time June said, "Pacific."

Meg didn't know where either of those were, and the other two women started bickering about why one was better than the other. Finally, Tia said, "June, Rhett will be at Coronado today. It's Friday."

"Oh, Rhett. Fine." June sighed again as if Coronado Beach was so inferior to Pacific, and Meg typed in the destination into her phone. A few minutes later, they'd found a parking spot and were tromping through the sand.

Which was so much better than snowshoeing in arctic temperatures.

But is it? her mind whispered. There, she had Eli and Stockton, wide open sky, and huge pine trees. She could feel God in the very Wyoming air, and she missed her former life for a few heartbeats.

But here, she had the wide open ocean, and new friends and a new job, and a very handsome man walking toward her. He slung his arm around Tia's shoulders, which made the normally business-like woman giggle in a very non-business way, and they continued through the sand together.

"Story on that?" she asked, pointing to Tia and Rhett.

"Oh, they're on-again, off-again," June said, watching as Tia kissed Rhett. "Apparently, they're on again at the moment."

Tia spun back to June and Meg, and said, "Meg, come meet Rhett."

He stood as tall as Eli, and he exuded just as much charm and confidence as the cowboy billionaire. "Nice to meet you," she said.

"Tia said you've come from Wyoming." He flashed a smile at her, and Meg flicked a look in Tia's direction.

"That's right. I was a nanny there." She hadn't kept her past a secret. She'd simply said she'd been looking for a change and the New Year was a good time to do it.

"She took care of a little boy named Stockton," Tia said. "Isn't that the cutest name ever?" She looked at Rhett with diamonds in her eyes and obviously, she was thinking about diapers and having babies with the man.

Rhett cocked his head and studied Meg for a second past comfortable. "Yeah, babe. That's a cute name." He turned away and settled onto the blanket Tia spread out, and Meg pulled a big bag of truffles out of her purse.

"All right, who wants salted caramel?"

June could've called all the dogs in the San Diego area with the way she shrieked, and Meg laughed as the treats were passed out. It felt good to laugh, to feel like she'd put in a good week's worth of work, and to be with people who had seen her the first time they'd looked.

SEVENTEEN

"WELL, WHAT DO YOU SUGGEST?" Eli practically threw the butter knife back onto the plate. "I haven't been able to do a single thing. There are no numbers in her phone. The top three locations gave me nothing. I've got *nothing*." The second time he said the word, it felt like the world had collided with the sun, and there was a fiery hailstorm beating through his body instead of a pulse.

"Well, I wouldn't hire a private investigator," Graham said darkly, shooting a look around the table at the other brothers. They'd all come to the ranch for Sunday dinner, and Laney had just taken the kids into the TV room to put on a movie.

"Why not?" Eli asked.

"Yeah," Andrew said. "Why not?"

"Do you guys even know Meg?" Graham glared openly at them now. "She won't like that. She left for a reason, and she covered her tracks really well for a reason too."

"Yeah, because she was mad at Eli," Beau said, forking up another piece of chocolate cake. Laney returned to the table, one hand on her stomach, temporarily drawing Graham's attention to her.

As Eli watched them interact, he couldn't help feeling like an outsider. A jealous outsider. He wanted what they had—and it burned that he'd had it once and lost it. Had it again and thrown it away.

"I have to get her back," he said, his voice raw. He'd been saying it for two solid weeks, and everything he'd thought of, from interviewing the hotel clerks, to searching for the top three locations she'd been on her phone, to logging into her social media, had led him nowhere.

And Graham had absolutely forbidden him from getting on her social media accounts. Eli had his own, and he'd been checking her accounts simply by watching, but she hadn't posted. Not a single status update in sixteen days.

She'd only been gone for twelve days, but it felt like Eli lost a little bit more of his soul with every passing hour. He had the money, and he could hire a private investigator. One who would go to the bank in Nevada where she'd closed her account and find out if she'd said anything about where she was going.

He'd thought about flying to various destinations surrounding Elko, but he couldn't imagine just running into his beautiful Meg in a city the size of Salt Lake or Vegas. They were huge, and it would take a miracle.

Of course, he'd been praying for one of those for twelve solid days, but so far, no luck. He really needed to start making his own luck, and hiring a private detective was one way to do that. And really, he didn't need Graham's blessing. Eli had his own bank account with plenty of zeroes.

"Do you have any mutual friends?" Laney asked. "Maybe one of them has heard from her."

Eli held his head in his hands as he thought about his life since meeting Meg. She spent most of her time with Stockton, and sometimes they went and did things together, the three of them. He had plenty of business associates, but did he have friends in the places he'd worked?

Bora Bora felt like it had happened eons ago, in another lifetime. And he hadn't left anyone significant behind there. He didn't think Meg had either. Before that, they'd been at a resort in Miami, and before that, he'd met and hired Meg in California, two days before he left the state permanently.

"She likes warm climates," he said, the thought just now dawning on him. She'd said she hadn't been in California for very long, and she was willing to relocate. Honestly, that single requirement had set her above the rest of the applicants, all of whom had wanted to stay in the Golden State.

He'd hired her because of that, not because of her qualifications or because Stockton liked her more than the others. So it was true, what she'd said. He'd always looked at her and seen her as only someone that dealt with Stockton.

He groaned and said, "I wish I could turn off my brain." The things he'd been thinking hadn't been all that nice. Problem was, most of the damaging thoughts were about him, and how he'd messed up all this time, and what he should've done. None of them were helpful, but Eli didn't know how to stop blaming himself.

Just like with Caroline.

He exploded out of his chair and said, "I have to go. Laney." He nodded at her, realizing that he was practically barking. "Thank you for the lovely dinner. Can Stockton stay the night?"

Just like when Caroline had died, Eli could hardly stand to look at his son. His eyes were too much like hers. Now, the sight of Stockton reminded Eli of what he'd lost, and why.

"Of course."

"Eli," Beau said, but Eli just shook his head.

"Come on," Graham said, standing too. "I'll walk you out." He didn't say anything to Eli on the short walk down the hall. Eli ducked into the TV room and pressed a kiss to his son's head. "I'm going home, bud," he said. "Laney said you could stay here for the night, and she'll take you to school in the morning."

"Okay," Stockton said. He'd been acting strange since Meg's departure too, and Eli couldn't blame him. It seemed like they were both a shell of what they'd once been with her in their lives. Without her, everything felt dark, and Eli had never been so lost.

Not even when Caroline died.

"You'll think of something else," Graham said. "I really don't think a PI is the way to go."

"How did you get Laney back?" Eli asked.

Graham drew in a breath and then pushed it out. "I made changes, Eli. I changed what had to be changed, and then I went and talked to her."

"Just like that?"

"Well, I made some big changes." Graham shrugged. "It worked out okay, I think."

More than okay, from what Eli could see. "I'd do that, Graham. If I knew where she was." Couldn't he see that Eli *had* to hire someone to find her? The world was a big place, and she could be anywhere. She'd cleaned out her bank account and hadn't used her credit card since withdrawing a few hundred dollars in cash at a couple of banks in town on New Year's Day.

And if Graham knew Eli had asked a buddy to look into that....

"You'll find her," Graham said.

"How?"

"I don't know. But I have faith you will."

Eli left, Graham's faith meaning a whole lot of nothing

to him. Eli had been to church twice now, asking anyone who'd look at him if they'd seen or talked to Meg recently. No one had.

As he drove back up to the huge, empty lodge, he finally decided to practice the faith his parents had taught him growing up.

He sat in the SUV and bent his head. "Lord," he started aloud. "I need to find Meg Palmer. Please. Help me find her."

He felt like he believed God could help him, but nothing happened. Eli went inside and down to the office, the only place that felt like Meg hadn't abandoned. She didn't spend much time in his office, so it had become a safe haven for him.

He opened his laptop and a moment later, a *bleep!* alerted him that he'd gotten some sort of message. But not on the computer. On his phone.

He tapped on the conversation bubble to find a Rhett Ahlred wanted to connect with him. "Rhett Ahlred." The name rolled off Eli's tongue and bounced around inside his mind. He almost declined, but then his memory jogged.

Rhett was a friend of Caroline's. They'd grown up together in Chula Vista, and he couldn't accept the message fast enough.

It read: *Hey, it's Rhett Ahlred from California. We met a few times through Caroline. Heard someone talking today, and it reminded me of you. Just wanted to say hello.*

"Just wanted to say hello?" That didn't sound right. In fact, those were the kind of messages women got from creepy guys. If this Rhett told Eli he really liked his eyes, he was out.

I remember you, Eli typed out. The man looked like California had treated him well. With nothing else to say, he hit send.

Sorry about Caroline, Rhett said.

Eli's stomach clenched. He definitely didn't need a trip down memory lane with someone he hardly knew. *Thank you.* His mother had taught him to be polite, and he'd do it once.

I heard someone use the name Stockton, Rhett said. *Didn't you and Caroline have a son named Stockton?*

Eli's internal organs rioted, seemingly moving around and rearranging themselves into painful places.

Yes. He hit send, his pulse bobbing from his temples to the back of his throat. It couldn't be the same Stockton. The name wasn't all that unique.

Yeah, I thought so.

That was it? Eli needed more information, and he thought the best way to get it was to simply ask. *Who was talking about Stockton?*

Oh, just a friend of my girlfriend's. A woman named Meg.

Eli dropped his phone, those last three letters burned into his retinas. Time slowed to a stop, and his mind stretched the words into long strands of sound.

A woman named Meg.

Everything rushed forward, and Eli stooped to pick up his phone, knocking his forehead against the desk. "Meg?" he dictated out loud as he typed. "Is there a way I can call you? She was my nanny, and I need to get in touch with her."

Rhett didn't answer, and Eli thought he'd just committed the equivalent of saying Rhett's eyes were beautiful.

Several minutes passed, and Eli paced the floor in the office, trying not to notice the coffee stain put there when she'd accidentally tripped bringing him a tray. But his stupid eyes gravitated to it over and over, reminding him of the sparks that had shot through his whole system when he'd touched her to help her stand.

Finally, another *bleep!* came from his phone, and Eli yanked it into eye range. It was just a number, and Eli couldn't dial it fast enough.

"Hey," he said when Rhett answered. "I hope this isn't weird. My son's just been dying to talk to Meg again, and I was wondering if you had a number for her."

"Nope," Rhett said. "But let me have you talk to my girlfriend, Tia."

ELI GOT OFF THE AIRPLANE, officially back in California for the first time since he'd buried his wife here. He stepped to the side, breathing suddenly so difficult.

He'd endured a full five minutes of questioning from Tia, who'd finally been convinced that Eli knew Meg and that he wasn't some creep. She'd kept in touch with him for a few days, and then finally said that they'd be at Pacific Beach on Friday after work.

Eli had promptly booked plane tickets for Friday morning, and now he was actually in the state he'd vowed never to visit again.

He'd begged Tia not to tell Meg anything, that he wanted to surprise her, that they'd been dating when she left, and he was trying to get her back. Tia, thankfully, was a romantic, and had been sending Eli tips all morning about the Meg she knew and what kind of flowers to show up with.

Eli knew Meg loved peonies, but as it wasn't exactly peony season, he'd have to make do with red roses.

He made it through the airport to the car rental. He'd been willing to come to the state to go on vacation with Meg and Stockton, and he wondered what she'd done with those tickets. As he stepped outside to get his car, he took a moment to think about Caroline.

"I'm sorry, sweetheart." The apology had been thought and verbalized several times already, but somehow now, it took a burden Eli had been carrying for far too long.

The sunshine in California seemed to smile down on

him, and he pressed his eyes closed and found peace flowing through him.

With Caroline almost fully cleansed from his mind, he grabbed lunch. Food was a good way to pass the hours. Then he bought flowers. He tried to keep his mind off the time, or what he was about to do.

He kept a prayer in his heart, silently pleading with God to give Meg an extra dose of forgiveness that day, to make her hours at work easy so she'd be in a better mood once he came face-to-face with her.

Finally—*finally*—Tia sent a text that said, *Leaving the office now. Thirty minutes, lover boy!*

Eli felt like he might be sick. But he got himself behind the wheel of the car and drove to Pacific Beach. He was ten minutes early, so he saw Meg when she unfolded herself from a dark blue vehicle, stretched her back, and looked out over the ocean.

Even from thirty yards away, she took his breath right from his lungs. Simply stole it. She wore a huge pair of sunglasses and a tiny pair of shorts, and Eli didn't think he'd be able to unseat himself and walk down the beach.

He certainly wasn't wearing beach attire, and he hadn't seen a single person in California wearing cowboy boots or a cowboy hat. He currently donned both.

She still wore her hair in an A-line, and Eli wasn't sure why he'd thought she'd look different. Only that he hadn't expected her to be quite so...Meg.

But she was. She was his Meg.

She smiled at her friends and collected a canvas bag from the trunk. The three of them walked through the sand and laid out blankets before settling down, their faces into the sunset.

Eli almost didn't want to disturb the peace she'd obviously found. But Meg got up again, launching him into action.

He practically tumbled from the car and slammed the door much too hard, drawing Meg's attention.

Don't stop, he told his feet. *Please don't stop.*

She'd slowed her pace, only going as far as where the sand met the sidewalk. She shaded her eyes, and Eli kept himself moving, moving, moving toward her.

"Hey, sweetheart," he said, stopping within reach of her and adjusting his hat nervously. She said nothing, and Eli's carefully practiced speech flew from his mind, leaving him silent and staring just like she was.

EIGHTEEN

A COWBOY ON THE BEACH. It was both of Meg's biggest fantasies rolled into one heavenly vision.

And not just any cowboy.

Her cowboy.

"What are you doing here?" came out of her mouth.

"I've been trying to find you."

"How did you find me?" Meg had done everything to make sure she could start fresh in her life, and there Eli stood. If he'd paid someone.... Her blood boiled though the sun wasn't that hot. "Did you hire someone to find me?" She folded her arms across her body and watched the guilt flicker across his face.

"No."

"You're not a good liar, Eli."

"I didn't, I swear. I wanted to, but—but Graham said not to. He said to have faith. So I did that, and the next thing I know, there's this guy messaging me, talking about the name Stockton, and a woman named Meg, and it was you." He wore hope in his expression now, that same insane hope Meg felt filtering through her body.

"What guy?" she asked, aware that her friends had stopped talking and were listening to every word being said.

"His name's Rhett, and—"

Meg spun back to the blankets where June and Tia lay. "Tia. What did you tell Rhett?"

The woman got up, a gigantic smile on her face as she came through the sand. "I didn't tell him anything." She linked her arm through Meg's and faced Eli. "Who's this gorgeous cowboy?"

Meg rolled her eyes. "Tia, you have a boyfriend."

"Sort of," Tia said, not taking her eyes off Eli. And dang, if that didn't make Meg angry. Tia could not have Eli. Eli was hers.

She startled at the way her mind still wanted to claim him, still wanted to be his.

"Rhett was a friend of Caroline's," Eli said, drawing Meg's attention right back to him. "He remembered the name Stockton and thought of us." He cleared his throat. "Of me and Caroline, and he reached out to me. After a few messages, it came out that he'd met a woman named Meg who used to be a nanny for Stockton." A smile touched his lips, there one moment and gone the next. "And it was you. I had faith I'd find you, and I did."

He cut a glance at Tia, who still gawked at him like he was a side of beef and she hadn't eaten in a month. "Can we talk privately?"

"Oh, of course." Tia unhooked her arm and turned to go back to the blanket. "But you forgot the roses, cowboy." She giggled as she went, and Eli's whole face turned bright red.

"Roses?" Meg asked, stepping onto the sidewalk. When he fell into step beside her, she tried not to be so giddy. Tried, and failed.

"It's a long story," Eli said. "I'll tell you later."

"How do you know there's going to be a later?"

"Meg." He paused and put his hand lightly on her arm. "Meg, I love you. I'm miserable without you, and I *see* you. I see you in my life for years to come. I see you at my side. I see you as Stockton's mom. I see you as my wife, my best friend, my everything." He swallowed, his nervous tell that made Meg's heart melt. "I can't live without you, Meg. Please, please come back to the lodge."

Meg liked the pretty things he had to say. She'd been waiting to hear them for a very long time, and she didn't sense any falseness in his tone or his expression. Eli really was a bad liar, and he wasn't lying right now.

"I can't come back," she said anyway.

Eli's whole countenance fell.

"I've just started a job here, and I really like it, Eli. I have friends, real friends." Her enthusiasm for her new life entered her own ears, and she heard how much she did like those things.

"You had friends in Wyoming."

"A few, yes, but this is different." Meg started walking again, and when Eli slipped his hand into hers, she accepted it. Squeezed his fingers. "I don't want to be Stockton's nanny and your employee. I won't," she said simply.

"What are you saying?"

"I'm saying that the only way I'm coming back to Wyoming is if we're married."

Eli remained silent for a few steps. Five, six, seven. "I have a few things to tell you first."

She'd heard him use this serious voice before, and she didn't like it. "All right."

"It's about Caroline." He didn't look at Meg, but kept his eyes glued to the ocean on his left. "She died in a car accident." He paused long enough that Meg wondered if he'd go on.

"I know that, Eli."

"Yes, well." He looked at his boots, then back to the ocean. "She wasn't supposed to be driving. She'd been sick, you see, and she was taking these pills that made her drowsy. But I was—I was—" He cleared his throat again, and then again, and Meg's heart started tumbling through her chest.

"Eli," she said, stepping in front of him and putting both hands on his shoulders. She waited, giving him a moment to find himself and then look at her. When he did, she said, "It's me, Meg. There's nothing you can tell me that I won't understand." While that might not be entirely true, it seemed to help him relax.

He nodded, swallowed, and said, "I was selfish. I didn't want to go to the store and get whatever it was we needed. I can't even remember now. But it was late at night, and it was something Stockton needed. So I—" He coughed and tried again. "I asked her to go. Said I was sick to my stomach, which I was. But I should've...she shouldn't have been driving." Tears welled in his eyes, but they didn't fall. "I killed my wife."

"No." Meg shook her head and slid her hands up his neck to cradle his face. "No, Eli, you didn't. Things happen. Things we don't understand."

"It should've been me in the accident."

"You don't know that. You probably would've taken ten times as long to find the item in the store." She didn't mean it to be funny, but a smile burst onto Eli's face, and a half-sob, half-laugh came from his mouth.

"Yeah, probably."

He really was hopeless in a grocery store, and Meg wrapped her arms around him. He was so solid, and so strong, and yet in that moment, she felt like the rock he needed to anchor himself to. And it felt really good to be that person.

"I came to California," he said. "I didn't think I could

do it, but I did. And I remember why Caroline and I lived here. It's beautiful."

Meg pulled away from him, a sudden understanding of all he'd done to find her shooting through her. "We were supposed to come to Disneyland together," she said.

"Do you still have the tickets?"

"Yeah."

"We can use them for our honeymoon." He leaned closer, his voice half a whisper when he said, "When I got off the plane, I didn't think I could stay. But then...it was like magic. I apologized to Caroline, and this weight I've been carrying disappeared. I feel free."

His hands landed on her waist, tucking her against his body. "I feel free to love you. Free to have a family again. Free to build a new future, with a new wife." The brim of his cowboy hat met her forehead, and Meg wanted to rip it off and kiss him senseless.

She held onto her patience and avoided looking at his mouth. "So you found closure."

"Yeah." His gaze turned thoughtful. "But you know what? I don't think I ever would've found it in Wyoming." He edged closer, his hat tipping back. "So thank you for leaving."

"I came here because I thought you never would."

"Glad to know you're wrong sometimes." His breath washed across her cheek, and Meg nearly went mad.

"Kiss me already," she whispered, and Eli swept the hat off and pressed his lips to hers in one swift motion.

From down the beach, June and Tia cheered. Meg giggled and then aligned her lips with Eli's again.

MEG WAITED ANXIOUSLY while the line rang. Finally the call picked up and Stockton's little voice came through Eli's phone. "Hey, Daddy."

"Hey, bud." The screen flickered, and then there he was, looking a little more worn than Meg remembered him.

She pulled in a breath as Eli said, "Can you see me?"

"Yeah."

"Look who I'm with." Eli shifted on the bench where they sat and tilted the phone so Stockton could see Meg.

The little boy squealed and laughed. "Meggy!"

"Hey, Stockton." Her heart pumped so fast, so fast. How could she have left him in the middle of the night? But she was glad she knew how to do hard things, how to follow through, how to get what she wanted.

"Where are you? When you comin' home?"

Meg smiled at him, sure he'd break a lot of hearts one day. He was already starting to talk like a cowboy, and if grew up to be anything like Eli, she'd have to beat the girls back with a stick.

"I'm in California," Meg said. "I live here now." While her whole heart wanted to return to Wyoming, she'd spoken true when she'd told Eli she would not be going back unless they were married.

"Daddy?"

Eli pressed his face in close to Meg's, and she thrilled at the nearness of him. She could definitely see the change in him since she'd left. He seemed...happy.

Meg had never thought Eli was unhappy, but seeing him now, she realized how much of a shell of himself he'd been. She'd only known him post-Caroline, and she'd thought that was simply how he was. But now that she knew he could be so much more, she loved him even more.

"Are you stayin' in California too?" Stockton's tongue tripped over the name of the state, and his bright blue eyes held worry and fear.

"No, bud. I'll be home on Sunday afternoon, like we talked about."

Sunday. Meg's heart sank, but she kept her smile hitched in place as the ocean breeze played with her hair. Eli certainly wasn't staying long. Of course he couldn't. He had a son, a job, a life, back in Coral Canyon.

Stockton glanced at Meg. "You can't bring her back?"

"I tried, bud." Eli cleared his throat, and Meg honestly hadn't heard him do it half as much in all the time she'd known him as he'd done it today. "But she says she can't come unless we get married."

Stockton's whole face lit up. His mouth rounded into an O but he didn't say anything.

"Shh," Eli said, and Meg pingponged her attention between the two of them.

"What's going on?" she asked in her best nanny-warning voice. "Stocky?"

"Can I tell her?" Stockton asked.

"No," Eli said quickly, but he was still wearing that smile that made Meg's stomach soft. She met his eye, but he simply grinned at her all innocently. But there was something going on here.

"Someone better say something," Meg said.

"Dad."

Eli gave an exaggerated sigh and leaned away from Meg. "Fine."

Meg became aware of him digging for something in his pocket, and then the edges of her vision blurred. What was happening? Was she ready for it to happen?

And then Eli had dropped to both knees, right there on the boardwalk, his feet extending out into the sand. "Meg Palmer. I'm in love with you. Will you marry me?"

She pressed one hand over her heart, just like she'd seen all the girls do in the movies. It just sort of happened, as if her heart was about to fly away and she wanted to make sure it stayed put.

"Say yes!" Stockton said. "And I can't see anything, Dad."

Eli held out a diamond ring, and Meg could certainly see the sunlight glinting off the huge gem. He lifted the phone with his other hand and said in a hushed voice that he wasn't trying to make too quiet. "She looks a little stunned, buddy. Maybe scared." Eli flicked his eyes back to her and then the phone again. "I can't really tell."

Stunned and scared summed up Meg's feelings pretty well, actually, and a giggle spilled from her mouth.

"Oh, she's laughing." Eli grinned and turned the phone back to her. "We love you, Meg. Please, please come back to us."

She looked at the ring as if that alone would make her decision. But she'd already decided. "Yes," she said, laughing some more as Stockton clapped his hands and Eli slid the ring on her left hand.

More cheering came through the phone, and Graham, Laney, and Amanda appeared in the frame, all smiling. Eli's mother wiped her eyes and nodded. Someone set a cake on the table, and then Celia's voice said, "Congratulations, you two. When's the big day?"

Eli lifted one shoulder, a clear indication for Meg to decide.

"Summer," she finally said. "Right here on the beach. And everyone has to come. California is amazing."

NINETEEN

SUMMER. Right here on the beach.

The words felt like barbs as Eli thought them while he stood at the window. It was cold in Wyoming; nothing like the golden light he'd experienced in California over the weekend.

And he was alone again, as Meg was holding to her promise that she would not come back to Wyoming until she was his wife. They'd spent hours talking things through, and she indeed wanted a beach wedding, in California, where she'd be living until summer.

Summer.

He'd pushed for the earliest date that could still be considered summer, and that was June first.

She'd agreed, but that date sat very far into the future for Eli—over four months.

"No way I can survive here for four months by

myself," he said to his partial reflection in the glass. The snow in the back yard seemed to mock him, and he seriously considered pulling Stockton out of school and moving the two of them to the beachside town where Meg had put down fast roots.

She'd claimed she couldn't abandon her co-workers at the law firm where she'd been working for two weeks. A hint of bitterness came with Eli's thoughts, and he swallowed to tamp it down.

After they'd ended the call with Stockton, she'd skipped through the sand to show her two girlfriends the ring. He'd met them both, and then he'd stolen Meg away from their Friday night beach relaxation.

He just didn't like that she'd chosen them over him.

"She hasn't." He sighed, trying to see the situation from another angle. From Meg's perspective. She deserved to be happy too, and she said she really enjoyed the secretarial work at the law office. "And now that Stockton is in school full-time, I might need something to do in Coral Canyon," she'd said. Then she'd leaned into him, gripping the collar of his shirt with both fists and looking at him with those dark, intoxicating eyes as she said, "Please, Eli. I just feel like I need to stay here and...find myself."

And he had no defense against her when she put herself in his arms and then kissed him with the passion she had after he'd said, "Yeah, all right, Meg. Summer. Here on the beach."

But now that he was back in Wyoming, without her,

he was regretting his moment of weakness. But he knew he wasn't really weak. Quite the opposite, in fact, as it had taken a lot of courage and strength for him to fly to California, face Meg, and set things right.

The phone rang, and Eli turned away from the window to answer it. "Whiskey Mountain Stables," he answered, wondering what was so great about being a secretary. Even he could answer a phone when it rang.

The caller wanted to book the lodge and the horses for a family reunion, and Eli managed to take care of business before he returned to his brooding. He should be working on some sort of proposal, but he'd been pretty useless around the lodge since Meg's midnight departure.

Tomorrow, he promised himself.

His cell chimed and he checked it to find Laney saying *You're still okay to pick up the kids?*

Yep.

And since Eli had to go to town later that afternoon to pick up Stockton and Bailey—a task Meg had done for a solid year without Eli even realizing how much effort it took—he called his mother.

"You want to go to lunch?" he asked her.

"Of course I do."

Eli smiled and shook his head at the cold, clear day outside the window. "Great, see you at noon?" He could waste a couple of hours with his mom and then sit outside the elementary school until the kids were finished.

And while he'd never done the dad thing all that well,

he found he liked sending his son off to school knowing what he was wearing and what he'd be eating, and he liked being the first one Stockton saw once class got out.

The boy talked to him more than he ever had before, and Eli was committed to being Stockton's caregiver more than Meg, even when she came back. It might've been wishful thinking, but he finally felt like he was in a place to be a dad.

He arrived at Salads Forever, his mother's favorite lunch spot and found her behind a giant bowl of greens at a corner table.

"You ordered without me?" He slid onto the chair across from her, very aware that he was the only human being with a Y-chromosome in the entire establishment. And wow, female eyes were heavy.

He ignored the gawking and looked at the berries and nuts dotting her lettuce. "I can't believe you eat that."

"Hey, *you* invited me to lunch." She grinned at him and speared a strawberry and a piece of what Eli guessed was spinach. He wasn't exactly sure, because he tried to avoid anything in the green food category.

"I hope you got me—"

"BLT, with an extra side of bacon?" The waiter looked expectantly at Eli, and he indicated the table in front of him. The man set the plate down, and Eli could practically hear the entire restaurant gasp as he picked up a French fry.

"And two cookies." The waiter placed another plate

on the table, instantly making the small space too crowded. Eli didn't care. For cookies, he'd make room anywhere.

"So, what's the occasion?" his mom asked.

"No occasion." He took a big bite of his sandwich so he could have time to think about his mom's next question. Because with her, there was always one more question.

"You come down to pick up the kids every day, and this is the first time you've invited me to lunch." She tactfully kept her eyes on her food. "You're engaged now. You've got to be happy about that."

"I am," Eli said around a mouthful of food. He swallowed and wiped his face with his napkin. Mayo in his beard wasn't something he needed the town gossip circles to circulate. "It's just...June first."

His mom nodded and put more salad in her mouth. She'd been such a big help to Eli over the years, and she always seemed to know when to speak and when to listen.

"I'm thinking of moving there with Stockton." Eli gazed at his mom, needing to judge her reaction. She yanked her attention to him, her eyes wide and everything stilling for just a moment.

"It's a bad idea." Eli peeled back the top layer of his sandwich and layered on his extra bacon. "I know it is." Everything in him sighed, and his mother didn't even have to say anything for him to know he better just get used to the next four months of living in the lodge without Meg.

❄

"COME ON, BUD," Eli said, the exasperation in his voice sky high. "This isn't the first time we've flown to California. Did you get your swimming suit?"

Stockton started digging through the fish-shaped carryon Eli had bought for him. They'd gone to visit Meg at least twice a month over the course of the last few months, and there were only two more weeks until the wedding.

"I can't find it." Stockton looked up at him like Eli could procure a pair of boy's swim trucks with a wave of his hand.

Eli was in no mood to parent today. That morning, he'd lost two clients who'd booked months ago, and now he had holes in his schedule for the stables. Laney had gone into labor last night, and he really wanted to be in Coral Canyon for the birth of his first nephew. But he wanted to see Meg too. Decisions had been made, but Eli didn't have to like them.

And Laney still hadn't had the baby, which only added worry to Eli's already frayed nerves. "We can buy a new one," he told his son. "Come on. Zip it up. We're going to be late."

At least spring had finally arrived in Wyoming, though the majestic Tetons just beyond the windows of the lodge still had plenty of snow on their tops. The drive to the airport would go quick without snow heaped all over, and as soon as Stockton zipped his bag, Eli grabbed it and headed for the door.

They made their flight, bought a new pair of swim trunks in the Long Beach airport, and met Meg on the beach where they'd be married in just thirteen days.

"Hey, beautiful." California really agreed with Meg. She had a golden glow Eli had never seen on her before, not even in Miami or Bora Bora. He realized now that it was more than the sun kissing her skin and making it bronze, but that she exuded joy that she'd never had before.

"Hey, handsome." She stretched up and kissed him while Stockton ran down to the water's edge. He loved the ocean, the sun, the water, and Eli considered once again the idea that he should simply move to California to be with Meg instead of having her come back to Wyoming.

"Everything set for the wedding?" he asked. "What can I help with?"

"Everything's set," she said, toeing the sand as she let him wrap his arms around her. She always told him that. Had not allowed him to give her a single dollar or know anything about the wedding itself.

She'd sent him several choices of appropriate suits he could wear that would go with her dress, and she'd asked him to pay for the family dinner after the ceremony. He'd told her he'd pay for all of it, whatever she wanted, anything. But she'd just said, *The family dinner would be great.*

"What about you and Stockton?" She stepped toward the blanket she'd laid out. In all their visits, he'd never seen her actually get in the ocean. She'd walk along the seam where the water met the sand, but she didn't swim despite wearing her suit. "You have your clothes and everything?"

"Yes, ma'am." He grinned at her when she rolled her eyes. "We'll be ready. Heck, we've been ready for months."

Meg flashed him a smile and picked up a bag of potato chips. "Couple more weeks."

He caught her looking at her engagement ring. "Did you talk to Taylor?" he asked. "Put in your two weeks notice?"

Meg took a long drink from her water bottle. "How are the stables?"

Eli looked in the same direction as her, finding Stockton a few yards out into the surf. "Just fine."

"That doesn't sound good."

"I lost some bookings this morning. It's fine." It wasn't like they needed the money. But Eli's pride was taking a hit. He'd thought he could make Whiskey Mountain Lodge into a fantastic mountain resort, where people would come and stay for the family charm, and the horses, and everything else he'd fallen in love with when he'd first come to the lodge Graham had bought.

"Doesn't sound fine."

Eli sighed and looked at Meg. He wanted her to be his biggest support, his champion, his sounding board. So he started talking, telling her everything he'd been doubting, all the ideas he'd had, and finally finished with, "What do you think I should do?"

Meg gave him the courtesy of remaining silent for a few seconds. She shielded her eyes as she looked into the sunset, though she wore sunglasses. "Well," she said slowly. "That little boy loves the ocean. And so do I. And maybe it's time you really consider leaving Wyoming." She looked back at him, and Eli nodded.

"I'll think about it."

"Pray about it," Meg said. "I think you'll know what to do then."

Eli kept nodding as he stood and brushed off his board shorts. "I'm gonna go help him build a sand castle. Apparently I promised last time we were here."

Meg giggled. "That kid has a good memory."

"Yeah, or he makes stuff up." Eli jogged down to the shoreline, and with his hands sandy and the shape of a castle starting to come together, he realized that Meg had never answered his question about whether she'd put in her two weeks notice.

TWENTY

MEG TWIRLED in front of the mirror, pure happiness cascading through her. A baby cried beyond the door, the sound growing louder as someone opened the door and slipped inside the bride's room.

Laney froze and sucked in a tight breath. "Meg," she said. "You look beautiful." She came over to where Meg stood in her wedding gown and gave her a big hug.

"Thank you for coming. How's Ronnie?" She twisted back to the closed door, the baby's wails pulling at her heartstrings.

"He'll quiet down quick enough," she said. "Graham's great with him." She put her arm around Amanda, and the sting of not having her mother there eased inside Meg. She'd invited her mom, but she didn't fly, and Carrie and Brittany had come without their families. Even her father had come all the way from Florida to walk her down the aisle.

The wind came in the open window, as this little cottage on the beach that was serving as their prep center didn't have air conditioning. Meg felt moments away from melting, and the ceremony didn't start for another half hour.

"Did you see Eli?"

"I sure did." Laney beamed at her.

So he was still here. Meg wasn't sure why she was worried he wouldn't be. She turned back to the mirror, determined not to allow anxiety or self-consciousness to ruin her day. She'd planned everything down to the smallest of details, and so far, everything was going off without a hitch.

Well, at least until she told Eli she didn't want to move back to Wyoming.

Her stomach swooped, and Amanda came forward with a gift wrapped in silver paper. "Meg, sweetheart, we're so glad you're officially joining our family. You and Eli are such a perfect match." She extended the gift to Meg. "Me and the boys and Laney put this together for you."

"Amanda." Meg's emotions felt like they were on a spiralizer, coiling and twisting every other second. "You guys didn't have to do this."

"I can't seem to get my other sons married off, so we really did." Amanda laughed, and Laney joined her.

Meg slipped her fingers under the paper just as the door opened again and her sisters entered. Carrie and Brittany were blonde and beautiful, the epitome of the perfect California beach babe.

She hugged them both and said, "I was just opening a gift from Amanda." She continued with the unwrapping and found a lovely frame inside, with a photo of a man and four young boys. Meg knew instantly which one was Eli— the one with the devilish glint in his eye and his chin tipped too low.

"Now my husband's here," Amanda said, her voice just a bit tight. "And you have something to start your life with." She indicated Meg should turn the frame over.

She did and found an envelope there. She untucked the flap and pulled out a gift certificate for a family photo session at a studio in Coral Canyon. Her throat and stomach both tightened simultaneously, but she managed to say, "Thank you. This is great."

"So you can get photos of your new family." Laney smiled at her. "And that's for the honeymoon."

Meg pulled out several hundred dollar bills and looked at the four women in the room. "You know Eli's loaded, right?"

"Oh, honey, this is for you." Amanda slung her arm around Meg's shoulders while Celia smiled at them both. "Don't even tell him you got it." She trilled out a laugh, and her emotions must've been riding a roller coaster with how up and down she was. "Now, come on. Let's put this veil on and get you over to the aisle."

Twenty minutes later, Meg stood just inside the flap of the only tent that had been set up on the beach. Streamers waved gently in the breeze coming off the ocean, and the sunset framing the altar and the rows of chairs facing it couldn't have been more picture-perfect.

Her father alone stood at her side inside the tent, and everyone else had gone to take their seats. She'd been texting and emailing her dad a lot over the past six months, and the renewed relationship had healed something inside her Meg desperately needed to fix. And she had.

"Dad," she said, turning toward him. "I don't know if I can do this."

He linked his arm through hers. "Of course you can. I've heard you talk about that man. Seen you look at him. You love him."

"I haven't told him I didn't quit my job."

Taylor had given her two weeks off for their honeymoon through Australia, New Zealand, and the Philippines, but come June fifteenth, she'd expect Meg back in the office.

Her dad swung his head toward her then. "Meg."

"I'm going to talk to him." She wrung her fingers together. "I am."

"When?" The incredulity in his voice rang in Meg's ears.

Eli had been carefully kept away from Meg as she'd made her way from the cottage to this tent, and even now, he'd been instructed to stand with his back to her until Graham told him he could turn and look. He stood very still, seemingly without a single nerve in his body doing anything but napping.

Finally, the wedding planner motioned to her, and Meg stepped out of the tent. She'd decided to go barefoot for the wedding, and her gown dragged on the sand behind her. But it was comforting and grounding to feel the sand between her toes as she walked toward where the wedding party waited.

They went first, concealing her. She caught a glimpse of Eli as he turned to watch the procession, and thankfully, he looked as nervous as she felt. With the bridesmaids and groomsmen standing to the side, Stockton made his way down the aisle, the official ring-bearer for his father.

Then it was Meg's turn, and her gaze locked onto Eli's and wouldn't let go. He seemed to devour her as she walked toward him, finally being passed over by her father and latching onto Eli as if he was her lifeline.

Because he was.

"Hey, beautiful." He leaned in as if he'd kiss her, and Meg pulled away.

The crowd twittered with laughter, and Eli's face flushed. "I'm messing it up," he muttered.

"Nope." She faced the pastor, but a voice was

screaming in her head and she turned back to Eli. "I have to tell you something first."

Eli flicked his gaze to the pastor too, and then to where his mom sat on the front row. "Okay."

Meg couldn't swallow, because her throat was so tight, and her whole chest ached as she hadn't breathed in several long seconds.

"You're freaking me out," Eli said, now completely focused on her.

"I don't want to go back to Wyoming," she said in a rush. "I didn't quit my job, and I think you and Stockton should move here." There she'd said it. Well, yelled it really, and the people around them started whispering.

Eli searched her eyes, shock and disbelief in his. "You didn't quit your job?"

She shook her head, her tears threatening to ruin the makeup Carrie had spent so long doing that morning. "Wyoming is cold."

A moment passed. Then two. What would he do? Cancel the nuptials?

"Say something," she said.

Instead of speaking, Eli tipped his head back and laughed. The sound vibrated through the cloudless sky, sending shockwaves through Meg. He motioned for Stockton to come stand by them.

"Stocky, Meg doesn't want to come back to Wyoming."

The little boy looked back and forth between them. "Okay."

Eli lifted his eyes to Meg's and said, "Okay," too.

"Okay?"

Eli faced the pastor and pretended to straighten the bow tie on his beautiful navy blue suit. He hadn't ditched the cowboy boots for the ceremony, but he was hatless, with a perfectly trimmed beard, and no wrangler belt buckle in sight.

"Yeah, okay," he said. "I think me and Stockton should move here too." He cut a glance at her out of the corner of his eye. "I just didn't know how to tell you, because I thought you'd *quit your job*."

Meg blinked at him and then she laughed too. "We're quite the pair, aren't we?"

"Not yet," the pastor said, a half-smile on his face. "Am I to assume the wedding is still on?"

"Yes," Eli and Meg said together, and Meg didn't care if they weren't married yet, if the pastor hadn't pronounced them man and wife yet, she tipped up on her toes and gave Eli a kiss right on the cheek.

"I love you," she said—well, pretty much yelled like she had before. The crowd really seemed to be enjoying this non-traditional start to the ceremony, because when Eli turned and took her into his arms, declared, "I love you too," and tipped her back for a much more passionate kiss than what she'd done, they ahh'ed and then started clapping.

When he finally brought her back to an upright position, Meg's whole face was hot and she couldn't wait to be alone with her husband.

"Can we start now?" the pastor asked, and Meg just nodded this time.

the end

SNEAK PEEK! HER COWBOY BILLIONAIRE BOYFRIEND CHAPTER ONE

ANDREW WHITTAKER CRINGED as the backdoor slammed shut behind him. Thankfully, there wasn't anyone around to reprimand him, but his childhood memories about not slamming the door echoed through his head.

His dad in particular had not been fold of all the loud noises, but with four boys in the house, some concessions had to be made.

The scent of warm hay and horse flesh met Andrew's nose and he took in a deep breath of it. He'd never considered himself to be a country type of person. Nor a man who could be content raising and riding horses.

But a strange sense of peace cascaded over him as he started the feeding. It was the same thing each day, and the thirteen horses that he and his brothers owned relied on Andrew to take care of them now that his younger brother, Eli, had moved to California to start a life there with his new wife.

Eli had bought most of these animals, and Andrew had *not* been happy to have them passed to him. At first. But now...now Andrew craved this early-morning animal care before he had to don the power suit and put on his public face for Springside Energy.

His older brother, Graham, was the CEO of the company, but Andrew had returned to Coral Canyon as the company's public relations director about a year and a half ago. He had the degree, and his brother needed him.

Honestly, the older Andrew got, the more he realized how much family meant to him. Especially since he couldn't seem to find someone to fall in love with and make a family of his own.

A cream and brown horse lifted his head over the door and snuffed at Andrew. "Hey, Wolfy," he said, reaching over to stroke the horse's nose. Eli liked Second to Caroline the best, but that made sense since his late wife's name had been Caroline. But Andrew had taken quite a liking to Wolfgang, and the horse always seemed happy to see him, and they'd spent a lot of hours in the mountains surrounding the lodge where Andrew now lived alone.

Well, not really.

"Bree's doin' okay," he told Wolfgang as if the horse had asked. The part-time interior decorator and gardener Graham had hired years ago had become full-time as she'd taken over Eli's responsibilities around the lodge with scheduling the horseback riding and other events at the lodge.

So much had changed in just the few weeks since Eli's wedding, with Andrew moving out of the basement and those rooms going up on the website for guests. Bree had moved into the room down the hall from Andrew, and he'd thought it might be awkward at first, with them being the only two living in the lodge now.

But it wasn't. He'd entertained an idea about asking her out for about five minutes, but there was no spark between them.

Plenty of sparks when she'd accidentally put a bowl with metal around the rim in the microwave and then grabbed it out with her bare hands.

"The bandages are almost off," he continued as he fed Wolfgang and moved down to the next stall. She still handled everything she needed to, because she could tap on a speaker icon and book groups for the theater room in the basement, or for horseback riding birthday parties, or whatever else she did.

Andrew wasn't sure what the events at the lodge were, honestly. He spent so much time at Springside, with its building about ten miles northeast of the town of Coral Canyon, that he rarely got home before dark. Even then, he'd stop by the kitchen for whatever Celia had left for him, and stumble down the hall to his bedroom. He didn't interact with guests or deal with much else at the lodge.

"Goin' riding today?" he asked Goldie, an older horse at the end of the row. "I know you are. Make sure you edge over closer to a child." The cream-colored horse was getting up there in years, which made her calm and approachable, but she couldn't go as far as she used to.

"I'm gearing up for the unveiling of Graham's robot. October first is the big day." Not that the horses in the stable knew when October would come, but Andrew had just over three weeks to get everything in line for the huge announcement about a robot that would hopefully make Andrew's job easier. Everyone's job should be easier with the invention that would be able to detect the gasses Springside mined without having to drill.

After all, the majority of the protests he dealt with stemmed from the drilling of the Wyoming countryside. His shoulders tensed and he hadn't even put on the fancy loafers or slicked his hair to the side yet.

He unconsciously reached up and pressed his cowboy hat on his head. He much preferred the simplicity of this life, and that had surprised him the very most about Eli's departure.

He finished feeding the horses, promised them he'd be back that night, and walked back to the lodge. The scent of coffee met his nose, and he said, "Morning," to Bree as he peered into the kitchen from the mudroom. He left his cowboy boots there and went to shower.

With the suit on, every crease exactly right, and his tie the color of watermelons with a white paisley stitched into it, he slipped on the expensive loafers and stepped into the bathroom. He sprayed the gel on his hair and combed it until it was just-so. He couldn't afford to be anything but personable and professional when he left the lodge for work.

Today was no different, though the tension in his chest felt stronger than it normally did for a Wednesday. He drove the ten miles to Springside in a nondescript sedan, just like he had for months. His route took him past the front of the building, where he'd turn and park in the back, behind a coded gate.

As he eased past today, the group of people gathered there made him groan audibly. Another protest. *Great.* Just what he needed today.

Andrew eyed a woman with slightly frizzy, light brown hair. She attended every single protest, and as she walked from person to person and said something, Andrew suspected she actually organized the demonstrations.

"It's fine," he muttered to himself as he turned the corner and headed for the back lot. If they didn't bother people, they could camp on the sidewalk in this early September heat wave Wyoming was experiencing. Andrew would keep an eye on them from his air-conditioned office on the sixth floor.

His morning passed with the chants beyond his window permeating the bullet-proof glass every half an hour or so. After a while, he didn't even hear them when they started up again, as he had a difficult article to respond to and a new blog post to write about the robot.

"How's the Gasman?" Graham asked as he came into Andrew's office.

"What are you doing here?" Andrew stood and gave his brother a slap on the back.

"I'm in the basement until next week. Only a few more weeks until we reveal this thing to the whole world." Graham swallowed like he was nervous, which Andrew knew he was. Graham had spent plenty of time in Andrew's office detailing how nerve-racking it was to have something from his mind splashed on the front page of newspapers and the covers of magazines—and worse, in little headline boxes with click-bait titles below.

Andrew was used to the pressure of journalism and dealing with the media. He had a degree in journalism and public relations, and he'd literally spent his adult life writing press releases, articles, and those Internet blurbs Graham hated so much.

"How's it going down there?" Andrew leaned against his desk, wishing he could come to work in jeans, cowboy boots, and an expensive polo the way Graham did. He looked polished and professional, and everyone knew who he was, but he didn't have to wear the suit to be in the electronics lab—or the basement as he'd taken to calling it because of the cold temperatures in the room.

Funny thing was, the huge, floor-sized laboratory was

on the third floor, nowhere near the basement of the building.

"It's going fine," Graham said, stepping over to the wall of windows behind Andrew's desk. "What are they mad about today?"

"It's been a while since they've been here." Andrew joined his brother. "I don't know what their problem is now." Only about thirty people had gathered on the sidewalk, and only a handful of them had signs. Weak ones too, scrawled on with thick, red permanent marker.

Red? Was that the only color in someone's purse?

He found the tall, slender woman with the frizzy hair. She'd pulled it back into a ponytail and carried a sign that read MAKE WYOMING FREE AGAIN.

He had no idea what that meant. It wasn't like the state had succeeded from the Union or anything. And Springside doing the hydraulic fracturing as they extracted the gases in the rocks beneath didn't bind Wyoming or its residents in any way.

He turned away from the window just as a swell of sound rose up from the crowd. He spun back to find the majority of them swarming a woman as she walked toward the building.

"It's Mom," he said, his pulse skipping around his chest.

"Mom?" Graham asked, peering out the window, but Andrew headed for his door. The protestors could march in their circles, chant their rhymes until they went hoarse, and then pack up and go home. But they could not approach visitors to the building, nor employees. The rules had been made very clear.

"Call Security," he said to Carla, his secretary. "The protestors are approaching a guest." He skipped waiting for the elevator and practically ripped the door to the stairs off its hinges. So maybe he was a little riled up because the guest was his mother. But she'd been through enough already, and she deserved to come eat lunch with her sons without having to deal with protestors at her late husband's business.

He burst out of the lobby to a wall of heat, suddenly wishing for those arctic conditions of the Wyoming winter, which he'd cursed for the entire month of February.

"Hey," he called, drawing the attention of a few of the people on the edge of the crowd. "Step away from the guest." He strode forward with purpose, his anger barely simmering under control. He was aware that thirty people had phones and anything he said or did could be recorded, put online, and shown to the world.

A tall, black-haired man emerged from the crowd, and Andrew really didn't like that he couldn't see his mother. "Who are you?"

"You know the stipulations of the protest on our property," Andrew said. "We allow you to peaceably assemble, but you aren't allowed to interact with anyone coming in or out of the building." He tried to see past the man, but he must lift gorillas for a morning workout, because he was impossibly wide.

"Security," a man called behind him, and the crowd dispersed then. Andrew darted into them, searching for his mother. It seemed like the arrival of security had caused a panic, like his team of four men could arrest anyone. They were simply bulky like that black-haired man, meant to break up conflicts with sheer intimidation.

Someone elbowed him in their flight, and he dodged left, only to be knocked sideways by another man. "Mom?"

He thought he heard her call his name, but he still couldn't see her. Someone moved, and there she stood, a look of determined fear on her face. Andrew took two steps toward her when he got struck with a protest sign.

He tried to stay on his feet, but falling was inevitable. Gravity pulled on him as pain exploded behind his right eye and down into his neck and up toward his skull. His right hand went to the injury, which meant he only had one hand to catch himself.

More pain in the knees and tailbone and wrist. Andrew honestly wasn't sure what was going on, but he knew blood dripped from his nose. He cradled his face, already imagining what the headlines would say and accompanying pictures would look like if he got photographed.

"Andrew." His mom reached him, and he grabbed onto her arm.

"Let's get inside," he said quickly, gaining his feet as

fast as possible. He kept his hands up to cover his face while a security guard ushered them inside and locked the doors behind him.

"This way, sir," Neil said, and Andrew didn't question his head security detail. He followed the beefy man down a hall and into the bathroom, his best suit already ruined.

BOOKS IN THE GRAPE SEED FALLS
ROMANCE SERIES:

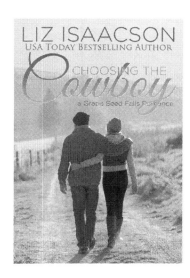

Choosing the Cowboy (Book 1): With financial trouble and personal issues around every corner, can Maggie Duffin and Chase Carver rely on their faith to find their happily-ever-after?

A spinoff from the #1 bestselling Three Rivers Ranch Romance novels, also by USA Today bestselling author Liz Isaacson.

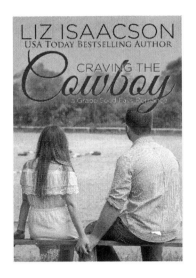

Craving the Cowboy (Book 2): Dwayne Carver is set to inherit his family's ranch in the heart of Texas Hill Country, and in order to keep up with his ranch duties and fulfill his dreams of owning a horse farm, he hires top trainer Felicity Lightburne. They get along great, and she can envision herself on this new farm—at least until her mother falls ill and she has to return to help her. Can Dwayne and Felicity work through their differences to find their happily-ever-after?

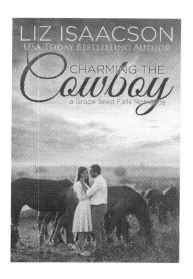

Charming the Cowboy (Book 3): Third grade teacher Heather Carver has had her eye on Levi Rhodes for a couple of years now, but he seems to be blind to her attempts to charm him. When she breaks her arm while on his horse ranch, Heather infiltrates Levi's life in ways he's never thought of, and his strict anti-female stance slips. Will Heather heal his emotional scars and he care for her physical ones so they can have a real relationship?

Courting the Cowboy (Book 4): Frustrated with the cowboy-only dating scene in Grape Seed Falls, May Sotheby joins Texas-Faithful.com, hoping to find her soul mate without having to relocate--or deal with cowboy hats and boots. She has no idea that Kurt Pemberton, foreman at Grape Seed Ranch, is the man she starts communicating with... Will May be able to follow her heart and get Kurt to forgive her so they can be together?

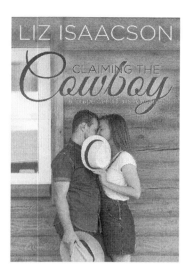

Claiming the Cowboy, Royal Brothers Book 1 (Grape Seed Falls Romance Book 5): Unwilling to be tied down, farrier Robin Cook has managed to pack her entire life into a two-hundred-and-eighty square-foot house, and that includes her Yorkie. Cowboy and co-foreman, Shane Royal has had his heart set on Robin for three years, even though she flat-out turned him down the last time he asked her to dinner. But she's back at Grape Seed Ranch for five weeks as she works her horseshoeing magic, and he's still interested, despite a bitter life lesson that left a bad taste for marriage in his mouth.

Robin's interested in him too. But can she find room for Shane in her tiny house--and can he take a chance on her with his tired heart?

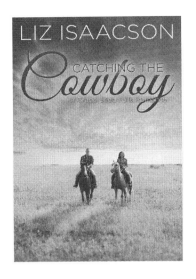

Catching the Cowboy, Royal Brothers Book 2 (Grape Seed Falls Romance Book 6): Dylan Royal is good at two things: whistling and caring for cattle. When his cows are being attacked by an unknown wild animal, he calls Texas Parks & Wildlife for help. He wasn't expecting a beautiful mammologist to show up, all flirty and fun and everything Dylan didn't know he wanted in his life.

Hazel Brewster has gone on more first dates than anyone in Grape Seed Falls, and she thinks maybe Dylan deserves a second... Can they find their way through wild animals, huge life changes, and their emotional pasts to find their forever future?

Cheering the Cowboy, Royal Brothers Book 3 (Grape Seed Falls Romance Book 7): Austin Royal loves his life on his new ranch with his brothers. But he doesn't love that Shayleigh Hatch came with the property, nor that he has to take the blame for the fact that he now owns her childhood ranch. They rarely have a conversation that doesn't leave him furious and frustrated--and yet he's still attracted to Shay in a strange, new way.

Shay inexplicably likes him too, which utterly confuses and angers her. As they work to make this Christmas the best the Triple Towers Ranch has ever seen, can they also navigate through their rocky relationship to smoother waters?

**Starting Over at
Steeple Ridge: Steeple
Ridge Romance (Book
1):** Tucker Jenkins has had
enough of tall buildings, traffic, and has traded in his
technology firm in New York
City for Steeple Ridge Horse
Farm in rural Vermont.
Missy Marino has worked at
the farm since she was a
teen, and she's always
dreamed of owning it. But her ex-husband left her with a
truckload of debt, making her fantasies of owning the farm
unfulfilled. Tucker didn't come to the country to find a
new wife, but he supposes a woman could help him start
over in Steeple Ridge. Will Tucker and Missy be able to
navigate the shaky ground between them to find a new
beginning?

LIZ ISAACSON

Finding Love at Steeple Ridge: A Butters Brothers Novel, Steeple Ridge Romance (Book 2): Ben Buttars is the youngest of the four Buttars brothers who come to Steeple Ridge Farm, and he finally feels like he's landed somewhere he can make a life for himself. Reagan Cantwell is a decade older than Ben and the recreational direction for the town of Island Park. Though Ben is young, he knows what he wants—and that's Rae. Can she figure out how to put what matters most in her life—family and faith—above her job before she loses Ben?

Learning Faith at Steeple Ridge: A Butters Brothers Novel, Steeple Ridge Romance (Book 3): Sam Buttars has spent the last decade making sure he and his brothers stay together. They've been at Steeple Ridge for a while now, but with the youngest married and happy, the siren's call to return to his parents' farm in Wyoming is loud in Sam's ears. He'd just go if it weren't for beautiful Bonnie Sherman, who roped his heart the first time he saw her. Do Sam and Bonnie have the faith to find comfort in each other instead of in the people who've already passed?

Learning Faith at Steeple Ridge: A Butters Brothers Novel, Steeple Ridge Romance (Book 4): Logan Buttars has always been good-natured and happy-go-lucky. After watching two of his brothers settle down, he recognizes a void in his life he didn't know about. Veterinarian Layla Guyman has appreciated Logan's friendship and easy way with animals when he comes into the clinic to get the service dogs. But with his future at Steeple Ridge in the balance, she's not sure a relationship with him is worth the risk. Can she rely on her faith and employ patience to tame Logan's wild heart?

Learning Faith at Steeple Ridge: A Butters Brothers Novel, Steeple Ridge Romance (Book 5): Darren Buttars is cool, collected, and quiet—and utterly devastated when his girlfriend of nine months, Farrah Irvine, breaks up with him because he wanted her to ride her horse in a parade. But Farrah doesn't ride anymore, a fact she made very clear to Darren. She returned to her childhood home with so much baggage, she doesn't know where to start with the unpacking. Darren's the only Buttars brother who isn't married, and he wants to make Island Park his permanent home—with Farrah. Can they find their way through the heartache to achieve a happily-ever-after together?

Before the Leap: A Gold Valley Romance (Book 1): Jace Lovell only has one thing left after his fiancé abandons him at the altar: his job at Horseshoe Home Ranch. Belle Edmunds is back in Gold Valley and she's desperate to build a portfolio that she can use to start her own firm in Montana. Jace isn't anywhere near forgiving his fiancé, and he's not sure he's ready for a new relationship with someone as fiery and beautiful as Belle. Can she employ her patience while he figures out how to forgive so they can find their own brand of happily-ever-after?

After the Fall: A Gold Valley Romance (Book 2): Professional snowboarder Sterling Maughan has sequestered himself in his family's cabin in the exclusive mountain community above Gold Valley, Montana after a devastating fall that ended his career. Norah Watson cleans Sterling's cabin and the more time they spend together, the more Sterling is interested in all things Norah. As his body heals, so does his faith. Will Norah be able to trust Sterling so they can have a chance at true love?

Through the Mist: A Gold Valley Romance (Book 3): Landon Edmunds has been a cowboy his whole life. An accident five years ago ended his successful rodeo career, and now he's looking to start a horse ranch--and he's looking outside of Montana. Which would be great if God hadn't brought Megan Palmer back to Gold Valley right when Landon is looking to leave. Megan and Landon work together well, and as sparks fly, she's sure God brought her back to Gold Valley so she could find her happily ever after. Through serious discussion and prayer, can Landon and Megan find their future together?

Be sure to check out the spinoff series, the Brush Creek Brides romances after you read THROUGH THE MIST. Start with A WEDDING FOR THE WIDOWER.

Between the Reins: A Gold Valley Romance (Book 4): Twelve years ago, Owen Carr left Gold Valley—and his long-time girlfriend—in favor of a country music career in Nashville. Married and divorced, Natalie teaches ballet at the dance studio in Gold Valley, but she never auditioned for the professional company the way she dreamed of doing. With Owen back, she realizes all the opportunities she missed out on when he left all those years ago—including a future with him. Can they mend broken bridges in order to have a second chance at love?

Over the Moon: A Gold Valley Romance (Book 5): Caleb Chamberlain has spent the last five years recovering from a horrible breakup, his alcoholism that stemmed from it, and the car accident that left him hospitalized. He's finally on the right track in his life—until Holly Gray, his twin brother's ex-fiance mistakes him for Nathan. Holly's back in Gold Valley to get the required veterinarian hours to apply for her graduate program. When the herd at Horseshoe Home comes down with pneumonia, Caleb and Holly are forced to work together in close quarters. Holly's over Nathan, but she hasn't forgiven him—or the woman she believes broke up their relationship. Can Caleb and Holly navigate such a rough past to find their happily-ever-after?

Journey to Steeple Ridge Farm with Holly—and fall in love with the cowboys there in the Steeple Ridge Romance series! Start with STARTING OVER AT STEEPLE RIDGE.

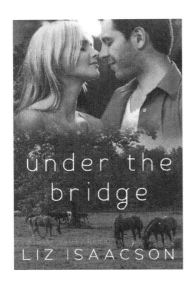

Under the Bridge: A Gold Valley Romance (Book 6): Ty Barker has been dancing through the last thirty years of his life-- and he's suddenly realized he's alone. River Lee Whitely is back in Gold Valley with her two little girls after a divorce that's left deep scars. She has a job at Silver Creek that requires her to be able to ride a horse, and she nearly tramples Ty at her first lesson. That's just fine by him, because River Lee is the girl Ty has never gotten over. Ty realizes River Lee needs time to settle into her new job, her new home, her new life as a single parent, but going slow has never been his style. But for River Lee, can Ty take the necessary steps to keep her in his life?

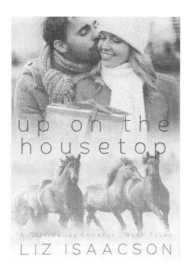

Up on the Housetop: A Gold Valley Romance (Book 7): Archer Bailey has already lost one job to Emersyn Enders, so he deliberately doesn't tell her about the cowhand job up at Horseshoe Home Ranch. Emery's temporary job is ending, but her obligations to her physically disabled sister aren't. As Archer and Emery work together, its clear that the sparks flying between them aren't all from their friendly competition over a job. Will Emery and Archer be able to navigate the ranch, their close quarters, and their individual circumstances to find love this holiday season?

Around the Bend: A Gold Valley Romance (Book 8): Cowboy Elliott Hawthorne has just lost his best friend and cabin mate to the worst thing imaginable—marriage. When his brother calls about an accident with their father, Elliott rushes down to Gold Valley from the ranch only to be met with the most beautiful woman he's ever seen. His father's new physical therapist, London Marsh, likes the handsome face and gentle spirit she sees in Elliott too. Can Elliott and London navigate difficult family situations to find a happily-ever-after?

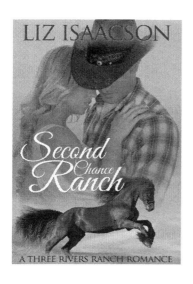

Second Chance Ranch: A Three Rivers Ranch Romance (Book 1): After his deployment, injured and discharged Major Squire Ackerman returns to Three Rivers Ranch, wanting to forgive Kelly for ignoring him a decade ago. He'd like to provide the stable life she needs, but with old wounds opening and a ranch on the brink of financial collapse, it will take patience and faith to make their second chance possible.

Third Time's the Charm: A Three Rivers Ranch Romance (Book 2): First Lieutenant Peter Marshall has a truckload of debt and no way to provide for a family, but Chelsea helps him see past all the obstacles, all the scars. With so many unknowns, can Pete and Chelsea develop the love, acceptance, and faith needed to find their happily ever after?

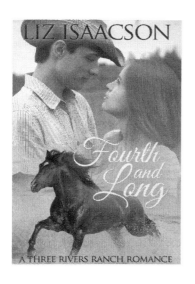

Fourth and Long: A Three Rivers Ranch Romance (Book 3): Commander Brett Murphy goes to Three Rivers Ranch to find some rest and relaxation with his Army buddies. Having his ex-wife show up with a seven-year-old she claims is his son is anything but the R&R he craves. Kate needs to make amends, and Brett needs to find forgiveness, but are they too late to find their happily ever after?

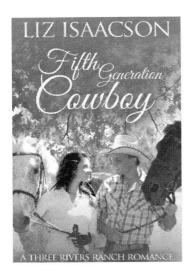

Fifth Generation Cowboy: A Three Rivers Ranch Romance (Book 4): Tom Lovell has watched his friends find their true happiness on Three Rivers Ranch, but everywhere he looks, he only sees friends. Rose Reyes has been bringing her daughter out to the ranch for equine therapy for months, but it doesn't seem to be working. Her challenges with Mari are just as frustrating as ever. Could Tom be exactly what Rose needs? Can he remove his friendship blinders and find love with someone who's been right in front of him all this time?

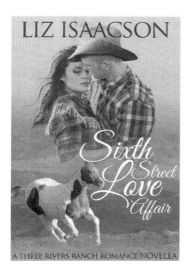

LIZ ISAACSON

Sixth Street Love Affair: A Three Rivers Ranch Romance (Book 5): After losing his wife a few years back, Garth Ahlstrom thinks he's ready for a second chance at love. But Juliette Thompson has a secret that could destroy their budding relationship. Can they find the strength, patience, and faith to make things work?

The Seventh Sergeant: A Three Rivers Ranch Romance (Book 6): Life has finally started to settle down for Sergeant Reese Sanders after his devastating injury overseas. Discharged from the Army and now with a good job at Courage Reins, he's finally found happiness —until a horrific fall puts him right back where he was years ago: Injured and depressed. Carly Watters, Reese's new veteran care coordinator, dislikes small towns almost as much as she loathes cowboys. But she finds herself faced with both when she gets assigned to Reese's case. Do they have the humility and faith to make their relationship more than professional?

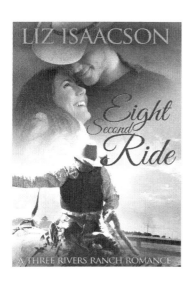

Eight Second Ride: A Three Rivers Ranch Romance (Book 7): Ethan Greene loves his work at Three Rivers Ranch, but he can't seem to find the right woman to settle down with. When sassy yet vulnerable Brynn Bowman shows up at the ranch to recruit him back to the rodeo circuit, he takes a different approach with the barrel racing champion. His patience and newfound faith pay off when a friendship--and more--starts with Brynn. But she wants out of the rodeo circuit right when Ethan wants to rejoin. Can they find the path God wants them to take and still stay together?

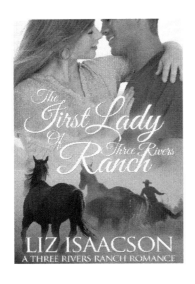

The First Lady of Three Rivers Ranch: A Three Rivers Ranch Romance (Book 8): Heidi Duffin has been dreaming about opening her own bakery since she was thirteen years old. She scrimped and saved for years to afford baking and pastry school in San Francisco. And now she only has one year left before she's a certified pastry chef. Frank Ackerman's father has recently retired, and he's taken over the largest cattle ranch in the Texas Panhandle. A horseman through and through, he's also nearing thirty-one and looking for someone to bring love and joy to a homestead that's been dominated by men for a decade. But when he convinces Heidi to come clean the cowboy cabins, she changes all that. But the siren's call of a bakery is still loud in Heidi's ears, even if she's also seeing a future with Frank. Can she rely on her faith in ways she's never had to before or will their relationship end when summer does?

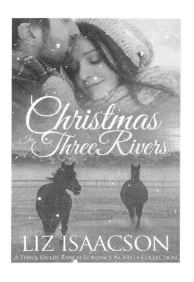

Christmas in Three Rivers: A Three Rivers Ranch Romance (Book 9): Isn't Christmas the best time to fall in love? The cowboys of Three Rivers Ranch think so. Join four of them as they journey toward their path to happily ever after in four, all-new novellas in the Amazon #1 Bestselling Three Rivers Ranch Romance series.

THE NINTH INNING: The Christmas season has never felt like such a burden to boutique owner Andrea Larsen. But with Mama gone and the holidays upon her, Andy finds herself wishing she hadn't been so quick to judge her former boyfriend, cowboy Lawrence Collins. Well, Lawrence hasn't forgotten about Andy either, and he devises a plan to get her out to the ranch so they can reconnect. Do they have the faith and humility to patch things up and start a new relationship?

TEN DAYS IN TOWN: Sandy Keller is tired of the dating scene in Three Rivers. Though she owns the pancake house, she's looking for a fresh start, which means an escape from the town where she grew up. When her older brother's best friend, Tad Jorgensen, comes to town for the holidays, it is a balm to his weary soul. A helicopter tour guide who experienced a near-death experience, he's looking to start over too--but in Three Rivers. Can Sandy and Tad navigate their troubles to find the path God wants them to take--and discover true love--in only ten days?

ELEVEN YEAR REUNION: Pastry chef extraordinaire, Grace Lewis has moved to Three Rivers to help Heidi Ackerman open a bakery in Three Rivers. Grace relishes the idea of starting over in a town where no one knows about her failed cupcakery. She doesn't expect to run into her old high school boyfriend, Jonathan Carver. A carpenter working at Three Rivers Ranch, Jon's in town against his will. But with Grace now on the scene, Jon's thinking life in Three Rivers is suddenly looking up. But with her focus on baking and his disdain for small towns, can they make their eleven year reunion stick?

THE TWELFTH TOWN: Newscaster Taryn Tucker has had enough of life on-screen. She's bounced from town to town before arriving in Three Rivers, completely alone and completely anonymous--just the way she now likes it. She takes a job cleaning at Three Rivers Ranch, hoping for a chance to figure out who she is and where God wants her. When she meets happy-go-lucky cowhand Kenny

Stockton, she doesn't expect sparks to fly. Kenny's always been "the best friend" for his female friends, but the pull between him and Taryn can't be denied. Will they have the courage and faith necessary to make their opposite worlds mesh?

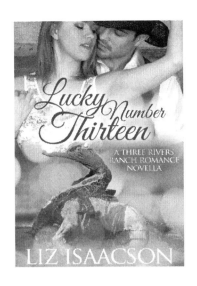

Lucky Number Thirteen: A Three Rivers Ranch Romance (Book 10): Tanner Wolf, a rodeo champion ten times over, is excited to be riding in Three Rivers for the first time since he left his philandering ways and found religion. Seeing his old friends Ethan and Brynn is therapuetic--until a terrible accident lands him in the hospital. With his rodeo career over, Tanner thinks maybe he'll stay in town--and it's not just because his nurse, Summer Hamblin, is the prettiest woman he's ever met. But Summer's the queen of first dates, and as she looks for a way to make a relationship with the transient rodeo star work Summer's not sure she has the fortitude to go on a second date. Can they find love among the tragedy?

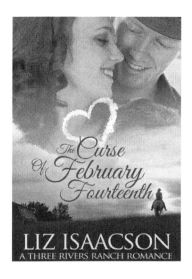

The Curse of February Fourteenth: A Three Rivers Ranch Romance (Book 11): Cal Hodgkins, cowboy veterinarian at Bowman's Breeds, isn't planning to meet anyone at the masked dance in small-town Three Rivers. He just wants to get his bachelor friends off his back and sit on the sidelines to drink his punch. But when he sees a woman dressed in gorgeous butterfly wings and cowgirl boots with blue stitching, he's smitten. Too bad she runs away from the dance before he can get her name, leaving only her boot behind...

Fifteen Minutes of Fame: A Three Rivers Ranch Romance (Book 12): Navy Richards is thirty-five years of tired—tired of dating the same men, working a demanding job, and getting her heart broken over and over again. Her aunt has always spoken highly of the matchmaker in Three Rivers, Texas, so she takes a six-month sabbatical from her high-stress job as a pediatric nurse, hops on a bus, and meets with the matchmaker. Then she meets Gavin Redd. He's handsome, he's hardworking, and he's a cowboy. But is he an Aquarius too? Navy's not making a move until she knows for sure…

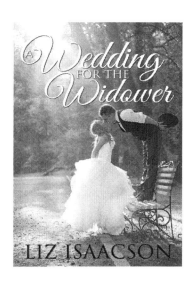

A Wedding for the Widower: Brush Creek Brides Romance (Book 1): Former rodeo champion and cowboy Walker Thompson trains horses at Brush Creek Horse Ranch, where he lives a simple life in his cabin with his ten-year-old son. A widower of six years, he's worked with Tess Wagner, a widow who came to Brush Creek to escape the turmoil of her life to give her seven-year-old son a slower pace of life. But Tess's breast cancer is back...

Walker will have to decide if he'd rather spend even a short time with Tess than not have her in his life at all. Tess wants to feel God's love and power, but can she discover and accept God's will in order to find her happy ending?

A Companion for the Cowboy: Brush Creek Brides Romance (Book 2): Cowboy and professional roper Justin Jackman has found solitude at Brush Creek Horse Ranch, preferring his time with the animals he trains over dating. With two failed engagements in his past, he's not really interested in getting  his heart stomped on again. But when flirty and fun Renee Martin picks him up at a church ice cream bar--on a bet, no less--he finds himself more than just a little interested. His Gen-X attitudes are attractive to her; her Millennial behaviors drive him nuts. Can Justin look past their differences and take a chance on another engagement?

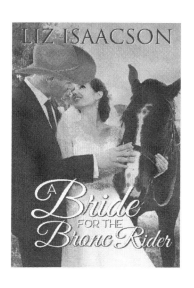

A Bride for the Bronc Rider: Brush Creek Brides Romance (Book 3): Ted Caldwell has been a retired bronc rider for years, and he thought he was perfectly happy training horses to buck at Brush Creek Ranch. He was wrong. When he meets April Nox, who comes to the ranch to hide her pregnancy from all her friends back in Jackson Hole, Ted realizes he has a huge family-shaped hole in his life. April is embarrassed, heartbroken, and trying to find her extinguished faith. She's never ridden a horse and wants nothing to do with a cowboy ever again. Can Ted and April create a family of happiness and love from a tragedy?

A Family for the Farmer: Brush Creek Brides Romance (Book 4): Blake Gibbons oversees all the agriculture at Brush Creek Horse Ranch, sometimes moonlighting as a general contractor. When he meets Erin Shields, new in town, at her aunt's bakery, he's instantly smitten. Erin moved to Brush Creek after a divorce that left her penniless, homeless, and a single mother of three children under age eight. She's nowhere near ready to start dating again, but the longer Blake hangs around the bakery, the more she starts to like him. Can Blake and Erin find a way to blend their lifestyles and become a family?

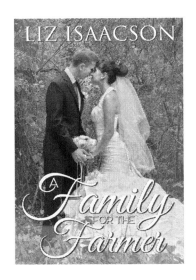

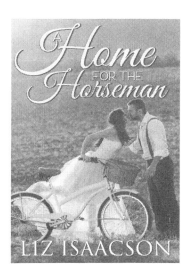

A Home for the Horseman: Brush Creek Brides Romance (Book 5): Emmett Graves has always had a positive outlook on life. He adores training horses to become barrel racing champions during the day and cuddling with his cat at night. Fresh off her professional rodeo retirement, Molly Brady comes to Brush Creek Horse Ranch as Emmett's protege. He's not thrilled, and she's allergic to cats. Oh, and she'd like to stay cowboy-free, thank you very much. But Emmett's about as cowboy as they come.... Can Emmett and Molly work together without falling in love?

A Refuge for the Rancher: Brush Creek Brides Romance (Book 6): Grant Ford spends his days training cattle—when he's not camped out at the elementary school hoping to catch a glimpse of his ex-girlfriend. When principal Shannon Sharpe confronts him and asks him to stay away from the school, the 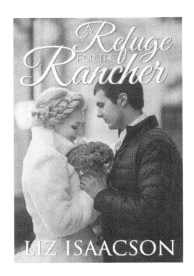 spark between them is instant and hot. Shannon's expecting a transfer very soon, but she also needs a summer outdoor coordinator—and Grant fits the bill. Just because he's handsome and everything Shannon's ever wanted in a cowboy husband means nothing. Will Grant and Shannon be able to survive the summer or will the Utah heat be too much for them to handle?

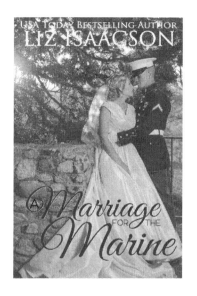

A Marriage for the Marine: A Fuller Family Novel - Brush Creek Brides Romance (Book 7): Tate Benson can't believe he's come to Nowhere, Utah, to fix up a house that hasn't been inhabited in years. But he has. Because he's retired from the Marines and looking to start a life as a police officer in small-town Brush Creek. Wren Fuller has her hands full most days running her family's company. When Tate calls and demands a maid for that morning, she decides to have the calls forwarded to her cell and go help him out. She didn't know he was moving in next door, and she's completely unprepared for his handsomeness, his kind heart, and his wounded soul.Can Tate and Wren weather a relationship when they're also next-door neighbors?

A Fiancé for the Fire-fighter: A Fuller Family Novel - Brush Creek Brides Romance (Book 8): Cora Wesley comes to Brush Creek, hoping to get some in-the-wild firefighting training as she prepares to put in her application to be a hotshot. When she meets Brennan Fuller, the spark between them is hot and 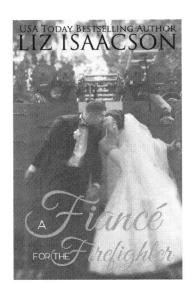 instant. As they get to know each other, her deadline is constantly looming over them, and Brennan starts to wonder if he can break ranks in the family business. He's okay mowing lawns and hanging out with his brothers, but he dreams of being able to go to college and become a landscape architect, but he's just not sure it can be done. Will Cora and Brennan be able to endure their trials to find true love?

A Treasure for the Trooper: A Fuller Family Novel - Brush Creek Brides Romance (Book 9): Dawn Fuller has made some mistakes in her life, and she's not proud of the way McDermott Boyd found her off the road one day last year. She's spent a hard year wrestling with her choices and trying to fix them, glad for McDermott's acceptance and friendship. He lost his wife years ago, done his best with his daughter, and now he's ready to move on. Can McDermott help Dawn find a way past her former mistakes and down a path that leads to love, family, and happiness?

A Date for the Detective: A Fuller Family Novel - Brush Creek Brides Romance (Book 10): Dahlia Reid is one of the best detectives Brush Creek and the surrounding towns has ever had. She's given up on the idea of marriage—and pleasing her mother—and has dedicated herself fully to her job.

Which is great, since one of the most perplexing cases of her career has come to town. Kyler Fuller thinks he's finally ready to move past the woman who ghosted him years ago. He's cut his hair, and he's ready to start dating. Too bad every woman he's been out with is about as interesting as a lamppost—until Dahlia. He finds her beautiful, her quick wit a breath of fresh air, and her intelligence sexy. Can Kyler and Dahlia use their faith to find a way through the obstacles threatening to keep them apart?

A Partner for the Paramedic: A Fuller Family Novel - Brush Creek Brides Romance (Book 11): Jazzy Fuller has always been overshadowed by her prettier, more popular twin, Fabiana. Fabi meets paramedic Max Robinson at the park and sets a date with him only to come down with the flu. So she convinces Jazzy to cut her hair and take her place on the date. And the spark between Jazzy and Max is hot and instant...if only he knew she wasn't her sister, Fabi.

Max drives the ambulance for the town of Brush Creek with is partner Ed Moon, and neither of them have been all that lucky in love. Until Max suggests to who he thinks is Fabi that they should double with Ed and Jazzy. They do, and Fabi is smitten with the steady, strong Ed Moon. As each twin falls further and further in love with their respective paramedic, it becomes obvious they'll need to come clean about the switcheroo sooner rather than later...or risk losing their hearts.

A Catch for the Chief: A Fuller Family Novel - Brush Creek Brides Romance (Book 12): Berlin Fuller has struck out with the dating scene in Brush Creek more times than she cares to admit. When she makes a deal with her friends that they can choose the next man she goes out with, she didn't dream

they'd pick surly Cole Fairbanks, the new Chief of Police. Not only is Cole twelve years older than Berlin, he doesn't date. Period.

His friends call him the Beast and challenge him to complete ten dates that summer or give up his bonus check. When Berlin approaches him, stuttering about the deal with her friends and claiming they don't actually have to go out, he's intrigued. As the summer passes, Cole finds himself burning both ends of the candle to keep up with his job and his new relationship. When he unleashes the Beast one time too many, Berlin will have to decide if she can tame him or if she should walk away.

ABOUT LIZ

Liz Isaacson writes inspirational romance, usually set in Texas, or Montana, or anywhere else horses and cowboys exist. She lives in Utah, where she teaches elementary school, taxis her daughter to dance several times a week, and eats a lot of Ferrero Rocher while writing. Find her on her website at lizisaacson.com.

Made in the USA
Columbia, SC
29 June 2020